HEAT OF THE MOMENT

BRIANN DANAE

MESSAGE

Gentle reminder... just because *you* wouldn't doesn't mean someone else can't. Also, this is fiction. Enjoy, and happy reading!

THOUGHTLESSLY
PASSIONATELY
IMPULSIVELY

LET'S STAY IN TOUCH

Instagram

instagram.com/brianndanae

TikTok

www.tiktok.com/@brianndanae

Facebook

www.facebook.com/brianndanae

Mailing List

https://bit.ly/BDWSubscribe

TRIGGER WARNINGS

-Strained parental relationship
-Mentions of death and grief
-Mention of stillborn (not on page)

PLAYLIST

If you're a music lover like me, enjoy the playlist I created to feel all the vibes while reading or after you're done.
Add it to your library, and enjoy!

Apple Music

Spotify Music

"HAVE FUN. LIVE A LITTLE."

ONE

"Another one?" Sovanna exclaimed, almost baffled.

She grimaced, watching Rea grab the bottle of 1942 *again*; it was about to be a long night. Grinning, Rea removed the cork and grabbed Sovanna's shot glass first. She poured a generous amount of Tequila while Sovanna frowned.

"Don't be that way." Rea smiled. Just one more, and then we can leave. You've only had one, anyway."

"You're lucky this is smooth." Sovanna accepted her shot like a champ and waited for her other friends to partake.

This was, in fact, a celebration for her, so she couldn't be a party pooper. Glancing around her packed-up apartment, Sovanna tried not to let her emotions ruin the evening. Lifting her glass, she smiled at her close circle of friends.

"Cheers to new beginnings, friend!" Diamond congratulated.

"It's not necessarily new. Just newer," Sovanna explained, and her other friend Ty sucked her teeth, waving her response off.

"Girl, we don' told you about being modest," Ty said.

"Right. Pop yo' shit." Diamond hyped her up.

Whether big or small, they never downplayed an accomplishment. No matter how many accolades or levels they reached, each one was celebrated. Sovanna still struggled with the fact that she'd made something for herself, so it was hard to accept their praises. She'd moved to Texas five years ago to pursue her career and had been thriving since. It wasn't something she should've taken lightly, and her girls would remind her.

Taking Diamond's advice, Sovanna tossed her shot back, the warm liquid making her body shiver. She was more of a sipper. Preferably a glass of chilled wine. Hitting the clubs hadn't been her thing until she moved to Houston, and she couldn't lie; she would miss the nightlife.

"That's what I'm talking about!" Rea cheered as Sovanna twerked to a rap song blasting through the portable speakers.

"That little skirt isn't going to make it through the night," Diamond chuckled.

Thankfully, Sovanna didn't plan on popping her ass at Club Vice the same way she did at home. The dark grey denim with oversized pockets was short, tight, and stopped right below the cuff of her cheeks. It gave off the illusion that she had more ass than she did, which Sovanna didn't mind at all. She was no longer the slim twenty-seven-year-old waiting for her grown woman weight to hit. Now, at thirty-two, Sovanna was thick where she wanted to be and toned where she felt mattered.

"I bet you it will," Sovanna replied, tugging upward on her black tube top that showed a sliver of her belly. "I'ma run to the bathroom before we go. Who's driving?"

"Mase sent the car service," Ty answered, speaking of her older brother, who owned his own transportation company. "They'll be here in fifteen minutes."

Nodding, Sovanna grabbed her phone off the counter and headed to her bedroom. Entering her bathroom, she flicked the light on and rushed to the toilet. Suddenly, her bladder was screaming at her. Once relieved, she washed her hands and checked her makeup.

The new foundation she bought earlier in the week melted into her deep brown complexion, giving it a glowing, smooth finish. Her knotless braids were styled in a cute updo with a few hanging while silver earrings dangled from her ears. Before she could head out and slide her heels on, an incoming call from her Mama interrupted her.

"Hey, ma," Sovanna answered.

"Hi, sweetie. What're you doing?"

Sovanna couldn't help but smile at her mama's sweet voice. It'd been calming her since she was a baby, and Mrs. Alicia still had that effect.

"Getting ready to go out with the girls."

"It is your last weekend in town. How're you feeling?"

Sovanna didn't want to get into all of that right now, but she knew her mama. She'd be worried all night.

"I feel blessed, ma. Honestly, it's bittersweet to be returning home, but I'm trying to embrace this new phase of my life," Sovanna answered truthfully.

"And I'm happy that you are. It's only temporary, but who knows... maybe you'll stay for good."

Sovanna chuckled. Those weren't her plans at all. "Mhm. We'll see. What're you doing up? It's past your bedtime, lady."

Alicia smiled. "Something told me to call you. Is that boy you've been dating going out with you all?"

Sovanna rolled her eyes at the thought of her ex, Josh. She hadn't gotten around to filling her mama in on their breakup, but she would soon.

"No. Just us girls for the night," Sovanna replied.

"That should be a good time. I just needed to hear your voice. Have fun tonight, okay? Live a little and be safe."

"I will, ma. Love you."

"Love you more."

Sovanna exhaled when the call ended. She didn't want to think about it being her last weekend in Houston, or she would get in her feelings. Stepping out of her bedroom after spritzing her pulse points and ankles with her favorite Louis Vuitton perfume, she walked back inside the kitchen and grabbed the bottle off the counter.

"Oh. Okay, then! Let me find out you had a change of heart in the bathroom, ma'am," Rea joked.

Sovanna smirked, poured another shot, and tossed it back. "I did, thanks to my mama. It's time to celebrate!"

Her enthusiastic mood was appreciated, making the girls take another shot with her. When their driver notified Ty that he was outside, Sovanna locked up, and they headed toward the elevator. She was going to take her mama's advice tonight and live a little. She wasn't quite sure what all that would entail but would certainly be testing it out.

EVERMORE
SERIES

"I'm so mad we didn't go to the concert," Diamond whined in Sovanna's ear.

The club was packed, and rightfully so. Once the concert ended, Vice became the after-party spot, and people came out in droves. A few well-known artists, such as Laurent, Misa, Renzo, and Draymo, had been touring for a few weeks and had to have Houston on the list. They showed nothing but love.

"And your coworkers are haters for not switching shifts with you," Sovanna replied.

Diamond couldn't get off work, but Rea and Ty had attended. Sovanna wasn't the concert type of girl anymore. Large crowds and excessive noise she couldn't control made her nerves bad. But she loved supporting her hometown and was happy to see their success. That's why she and her friends were in a section singing along to Laurent's newest single, *Show Me Something*, as if they'd written the lyrics for him.

Sovanna swayed from side to side, snapping her fingers and bobbing her head to the smooth R&B beat. Even though the club was packed, everyone was vibing and she hoped it remained that way. There was nothing worse than going out to have a good time, and grown adults behaving like children ruined the night.

Taking in her surroundings, Sovanna admired the women in the section next to them turning up. Bottle girls weaved through the crowd with marquee letter signs lighting up the area and requested bottles from different parties. When a group of them headed toward their section holding a sign that read 'Congratulations Vanna!' Sovanna's face lit up.

"Oh my gosh," she whispered, smiling at her friends who had their phones out recording her.

A bottle of 1942 Don Julio was placed on their table, along with a carafe of orange juice and a bucket of ice. She beamed harder under the flashing lights as the DJ gave her a shoutout.

"We got a few folks we're celebrating tonight.

Congrats to Ms. Vanna up top!" The DJ shouted into the mic, making Sovanna blush.

He continued with his celebratory shoutouts while Sovanna hugged her friends. She wasn't the emotional friend of the crew, but they were trying to make her be. Having a group of women who not only supported her but showed up for her in ways her own family didn't brought tears to Sovanna's eyes.

"Awww. Not you tearing up," Diamond cooed.

Sovanna fanned her face and smirked. "An eyelash must've gotten in my eye. Thank y'all so much." She gave them all hugs and then looked down at the bottle. "Um, who's drinking this?"

Ty chuckled. "We are. It's still early. Pour up, friend!"

On cue, the DJ played Tomorrow 2 by GloRilla and Cardi B. Sovanna found herself jigging to the beat and rapping Glo's verse word for word after taking a shot.

"Get it, Vanna!" Rea hyped.

Buzzing and feeling good, she vowed that this was her last drink for the night. She wasn't drunk but would most definitely be if she didn't slow down. After dancing through two songs, Sovanna sat down and grabbed one of the unopened bottles of water.

After quenching her thirst, her eyes roamed the club.

If she didn't have plans to return to her hometown next week, she would've gladly exchanged numbers with a few of the men in attendance. After being in a relationship for almost two years, Sovanna didn't mind dipping her foot into the dating scene again. That's all it could be, though. With her new promotion and recent breakup, casual dating was all she had to offer.

"Vanna," Rea sang, grabbing her attention.

Sovanna's head swiveled. "What's up, honey?"

Rea draped her arm over her shoulder and grinned. "It's your last night out, so I feel it's only right we play one last game of truth or dare."

Shaking her head, Sovanna tried removing her arm from around her. "Why now?" She whined. "Can't we wait until brunch tomorrow?"

"No, ma'am. It's now, or I'm taking my gift back."

Sovanna gasped, making Rea laugh. "I wish you would take my Chanel purse back."

At the go-away dinner they gave Sovanna, her friends didn't miss a beat with their parting gifts. They were so proud of her accomplishments and wanted her to know it. Sovanna loved all of her gifts, but it was truly the thought that counted for her. Her girls had gone the extra mile to make her last weekend extra special. So, she figured the least she could do was accept Rea's request.

Playing truth or dare on a whim when they were out started about a year ago. On one occasion, they dared Ty to reach out to a man who looked just like her incarcerated father. She came across his page on Instagram and could've sworn she was looking at the younger version of her daddy. One dare turned into Ty messaging Mase, asking who he was related to, and the rest was history. He'd been spoiling her ever since, and Rea was now connected to her extended family.

More good than bad had come from them playing the game, and plenty of laughs had been shared, so Sovanna took the bait. After all, it was her last night out.

"So, what's it gonna be?" Rea questioned.

Not in the mood to reveal any truths, Sovanna opted for the latter. "Dare."

Rea grinned and happily clapped her hands. "Oooh. Okay, okay. Let's see. I dare you to pick a man in here and have a one-night stand."

Sovanna's wide-set eyes expanded. "Rea," she groaned. "Out of all the things, you had to choose that?"

"What y'all over here talking about?" Diamond asked, noticing Sovanna's disturbed facial expression.

Rea smirked. "I dared her to have a one-night stand."

"And you know what happens if you decline the dare," Ty said with a smirk as she walked up.

Sovanna playfully rolled her eyes. She declined the last dare that would've forced her to reach out to her ex and tell him she wanted to make things work. In the end, she was out of one hundred and fifty dollars, each woman receiving fifty. Money wasn't the issue. Sovanna didn't like to lose. Reaching out to her ex was an absolute hell no, though, and she gladly sent them their money through Zelle.

"Fine," Sovanna huffed, then smiled. "I mean... I've never had one, so I guess this is perfect timing."

"Exactly! That's the spirit," Rea encouraged.

"Plus, half the niggas in here are probably from out of town anyway. You'll never see him again," Diamond added.

She had a point. People traveled to the city for the weekend all the time, then returned home, letting whatever happened in Houston stay in Houston. Ironically, Sovanna was returning home, so even if they lived in the city, she would no longer live here to see them.

"True," Sovanna mumbled, eyeing the men in the section next to them.

They were handsome, and only one stood out from the group of six, but not enough to make Sovanna approach him. Plus, the way he had his hat cocked to the side bothered her. If she was going to live a little like her mama suggested, she wanted a man that made her mouth water and pussy clench upon first sight.

"He's fine as hell, girl," Rea said, eyeing the man who looked like he could be a basketball player due to his height.

"Yeah, he is. But he's finer, though," Sovanna suggested, nodding toward the man who captured her eyes.

Her attention was focused on the section near the stage, where every man standing alongside the R&B sensation Laurent garnered attention with ease. A crew of fine-ass men was just as dangerous as a friend group of fine-ass women, but Sovanna was willing to walk on the wild side. For once in a long time, she placed her inhibitions in an imaginary box and locked it. She'd worry about finding the key to retrieve them when morning came.

With the stage to the left of them, Sovanna had a clear view of her prey, but she wanted to get closer. She watched him for another song, admired how folks who walked up on the stage greeted him, and felt her heart stop when he smiled at something Laurent said to him. The way her potential one-night-stand man was finessing his thick beard and bobbing his head in a relaxed manner intrigued her. A laid-back man had always been her type, and Sovanna hoped she hadn't pegged him wrong.

"You nervous?" Rea asked.

Sovanna shook her head. "No. Was just waiting on the perfect timing. How do I look?"

Rea gave her a once over, adjusted her tube top, and handed her a mint. "Like a bad bitch who needs some dick. We'll be here watching and waiting."

Chuckling, Sovanna applied a new coat of lip gloss and headed out of their section. She carefully made it down the steps and confidently moved through the crowd to the stage. The section Mr. Tall Dark and Handsome stood in was roped off, and security posted up outside of it.

Sovanna noticed the women occupying the plush couches with their legs crossed and flutes of liquor in their hands, cutely enjoying the vibes. The men, fine-ass men dressed in designer threads, clouded the space with potent weed smoke. The man she came over to address locked curious eyes with her, making Sovanna almost rethink her decision.

Damn you, Rea, she fussed to herself. His eyes stayed trained on her, wondering who she was and who she knew. He was used to women of all calibers using their beauty and charm to get whatever they wanted, but not many succeeded with him. Sovanna had him reconsidering, though. In the six seconds it took for her to pass his viewpoint and access the steps, she'd piqued his interest.

"Section is full, Ms. Lady," the security guard said, obstructing her view.

Sovanna smiled politely. "I won't take up too much space."

"No can do. Maybe next time," he said.

"There won't be a next time," she replied, keeping a smile on her face.

One more decline and she was heading back to their section. Sovanna wasn't pressed for an interaction, nor did she care to feel the sting of the embarrassment she knew would come if he turned her away. The security guard stood his ground, giving her a stern look.

"Can you just tell the guy with the," she began,

peeking around his large frame to see what the man had on. "Oh. Never mind."

Much to her surprise, the man of the hour walked their way, forcing the security guard to scoot to the side. He was as tall as the burly man who denied her access, with a thick-framed body that made her mouth water. She craned her neck to take him in under the dimly lit area.

Sovanna couldn't make out all his features, but his manicured beard perfectly outlined his chiseled jaw. It was luscious, giving a touch of ruggedness to his polished appearance. The few strands of gray that she detected added an air of maturity that she loved. When he spoke, his smooth voice caressed her being like the silk pillowcases she slept on.

"What seems to be the issue, gorgeous?" He questioned, bending to speak in her ear.

The warmth and gentleness of his voice drew Sovanna in without effort. Her eyes lightly rolled at the smell of his heady cologne. The rich, musky yet earthy, powdery scent and minty fresh breath made her momentarily lose her train of thought.

"May I speak with you for a moment?"

"Am I in trouble?" He asked, leaning back to look into her upturned brown eyes.

She giggled at his joking tone. The smirk on his

face made her want to hump it right off. He wasn't in trouble *yet*.

"No. Not if you don't want to be," she replied.

Curious about the woman before him, he stood straight and spoke to the security guard before taking the four steps down. He put his hand out for Sovanna to take, making her do the same.

Okay. A gentleman, she thought.

Looking over her shoulder, she gave her girls a thumbs up, indicating she was good. Thankful that he hadn't given her a hard time, Sovanna let him guide her to a quieter area of the club. He towered over her a good five inches with her heels on, so he had to be at least six-foot-four. Sovanna wanted to climb him and ask if he were an NFL player while doing so.

He waved a card over the keyless entry when they approached a door, gaining access. She could still feel the bass in her chest as the motion sensor lights to the office they entered popped on. Sovanna wanted to fake intrigue about the massive space and impressive décor, but he, whose name she was dying to know, stole her attention. She hoped he didn't have any nefarious intentions with bringing her back here because that would surely ruin his image.

His attire for the night was a Rhude +

Lamborghini black short-sleeved button-down, black denim, and coconut milk-colored Forces. She was thankful for the bright lighting and took in his beyond-handsome face of rich, cocoa brown. Bushy, untamed brows laid atop downturned, pensive, lighter brown eyes. Sovanna couldn't stop staring at his lips. They were the perfect balance between full-ness and definition, the top slightly darker than the juicy bottom lip.

Her eyes drifted to his large hands that were crossed in front of him as he leaned against the black desk. The thick veins in his hands made Sovanna's pulse quicken and brain clutter with disgusting thoughts. Thoughts that made her rashly follow him into this office. Her eyes dropped to his fingernails — the ones she could see. They were clean like his low, crisp cut with deep waves. The man was fine as fuck, smelled good, and had Sovanna at a loss for words when there had been so many she wanted to say minutes prior.

"As much as I'd love to stare at you for the rest of the night, I have things to do, gorgeous. What was so urgent that you needed to pull me away?"

His soothing, deep voice snapped her out of the trance she'd been placed in.

"This may sound crazy, or maybe not, but I want to have a one-night stand with you."

He licked his lips, making Sovanna inhale slowly.

"Are you under the influence?"

"Not quite."

"So, you're purely bold like this all the time?" He questioned; head cocked to the left. Amusement danced in his eyes.

Sovanna chuckled. "No. Should I be intoxicated?"

"Not at all. I want you to consent to everything that goes down tonight if I agree. With the way you're standing there eye-fucking me, I'ma need you to be fully coherent *if* I slide my dick up in you."

Heat engulfed her frame, and for a split second, Sovanna wondered if she'd gotten in over her head. This man was of a different caliber, but she figured he would be. It was the reason she spotted him so easily out of the crowd.

"So, you agree?" She asked.

He smirked. "On one condition. Matter of fact, two."

Sovanna's right brow quirked. "I'm listening."

"We exchange names, and then you tell me the

quickest way you want me to make you cum right now."

Her lashes fluttered as she rapidly blinked. His requests, one of them at least, caught her completely off guard. That alone should've warned Sovanna that he was a walking red flag, yet all she wanted him to do was use it to bind her wrists while he ate her pussy from the back. *That* was the quickest way to make her climax.

Wanting to test her imagination, Sovanna stepped closer to him and stuck her hand out. "My name is Loren."

He figured she wasn't being truthful, but that was fine with him. With no plans but to break her back in and send her on her way, she could tell him anything. Specifically, the answer to his second request. Stepping into her space, he took her hand and shook it.

"Pleasure to meet you, Loren," he spoke calmly before turning her body to face the desk.

Gently, he pushed her forward, making her chest rest against the cold marble, with her arms outstretched before her and wrists clasped in his right hand. Sovanna's breathing picked up when she felt his bulge against her backside and warm breath against her neck.

"My name is Zahir," he introduced, kissing her shoulder.

Her eyes fluttered, and her vaginal muscles contracted. The action was intimate and far more than what Sovanna had prepared for. His name suited him perfectly. It was masculine and seductive. Sovanna was already thinking of how she would sound moaning it.

"May I lift your skirt?" He asked, and she nodded. "Use your words. Let me hear you say yes."

"Yes," she rushed out in a breathy manner.

She was so turned on, Zahir could've asked her to do anything right about now, and she would've said yes. Floetry didn't have shit on her. With permission, he raised her skirt, which was already halfway over her ass, and caressed her cheeks. Giving the right one a smack, he reminded her of their agreement.

"Tell me what I need to hear, Loren, or I'm walking out of that door."

His dominance didn't bother her at all. Technically, this is what she asked for, so she obliged and widened her legs. Zahir wasn't the type of man who readily agreed to a one-night stand, yet he couldn't recall ever being approached the way Sovanna had. Fucking her in the club wasn't on his agenda, but sampling the treasure between her thighs was. Only a woman with some good-ass pussy could boldly proposition him for sex, and he wanted to find out how good.

"I want you to eat it from the back," she said softly.

Zahir lifted her onto the desk with ease, forcing Sovanna to spread her legs.

"Thank you for answering me. Now, arch that fucking back."

Sovanna's sticky thong was pulled to the side, and Zahir's warm, thick tongue took its place. A million and one thoughts ran through Sovanna's mind, and he wasted no time licking and slurping them out of her. The first lick caused her to gasp loudly, while the suction of his plush lips against her clit had her moaning his name.

"Zahir," she called out softly.

His name falling from her lips sounded heavenly. It was as if she were the only one that was meant to say it in every octave. Zahir wanted her to shout it like she was upset. He spread her lips, loving the fact that she was a creamer. She dripped onto his silky beard, but Zahir didn't care. He licked up the delicious mess and zoned in on her engorged clit.

Up and down, his tongue flicked against her.

Sovanna's legs trembled. She hadn't had sex in months and had gone even longer without oral pleasure. Zahir sucked on her pussy like he was trying to win a medal. A fucking gold medallion that he'd hang up with the rest of the awards he received for eating pussy like a champion. A damn manic who couldn't get enough of Sovanna's sweet taste.

"Mmm," Sovanna moaned, rotating her hips, riding the wave of his tongue.

Zahir didn't speak when devouring his meal. He ate in peace, grunting and groaning every so often to showcase his pleasure. His tongue twirled before latching onto her nub, bringing Sovanna to her peak.

Her stomach clenched simultaneously with her walls. The pressure was so intense that a blur of stars and vibrant colors danced behind her lids as she climaxed. Zahir didn't just eat her pussy; he cleaned the plate. Licked the mothafucka off the bone and sucked his teeth when finished.

"Oh, my gosh!" Sovanna shrieked as he continued pleasuring her.

Dinner had been served and devoured, and now he wanted something a little sweeter. Sovanna's second orgasm snuck up on her so quickly, she scooted up the desk and laid out on it in satisfaction and exhaustion.

Smack!

Smack!

Smack!

The smacks to her ass swayed her none. Neither did his passionate kisses to each cheek.

"You have some grade-A pussy on you, Ms. Loren. The night's still young, and my dick is hard, but I refuse to fuck you in this office. Once you get yourself cleaned up, grab the extra room key beside you. I'm staying at the Elysian."

Those were his parting words as he adjusted her thong back in place and lowered her skirt. Sovanna turned her head to glance at him and caught the most erotic sight she'd ever seen. Zahir had no plans on washing the remnants of her from his face. He simply dragged a hand over his mouth and rubbed her juices into his beard as if it were an organic oil. He was adding Sovanna's essence into his regimen only for the night.

After washing his hands in the connected bathroom before leaving the office, Zahir glanced at Sovanna as she slid one of her heels back on. In less than fifteen minutes, he'd brought her back-to-back orgasms and didn't think twice about giving her a key to his room. He surmised that she wasn't from here, and neither was he. If she showed up to his room, he promised to make this one-night stand one she would remember forever.

2

TWO

When Sovanna's mama told her to live a little, she was one hundred percent sure she didn't mean for her to get slutted out in the office of a club by a fine-ass man.

She should've been clearer with her advice. Technically, they weren't strangers since names and bodily fluids had been exchanged. Sovanna wasn't keeping up with the textbook definition. All she knew was that the man ate her pussy like he'd known her his entire life. He followed instructions extremely well and gave them with just as much authority.

After cleaning herself up in the office, Sovanna returned to their section and tried to act as normal as possible. Not wanting to even make eye contact with Zahir on her way back, she took a different route back to her girls. Little did Sovanna know Zahir had already exited the club. On his way out, he made a pit stop.

"How you ladies doing tonight?" Zahir questioned, entering their section.

They all gave him a once-over.

"We're fine. Where's our friend?" Rea questioned.

Zahir smirked. "She'll be out shortly. I just wanted to let y'all know she's in good hands for the night. Don't worry about the bill. It's on the house. Enjoy y'all evening."

"Oop. Well, okay then." Diamond chuckled. "Thank you!"

His head bobbed forward before he weaved through the crowd.

On wobbly legs, Sovanna returned to their section two minutes later and plopped down on the couch. The content smile on her face made her girls crack up.

"You busted it open in the office?" Rea asked in a whisper.

All Sovanna could do was nod her head. "Not all the way."

"What the hell does that mean?" Diamond asked, laughing.

"From the glossed look in her eyes, that man put his face all between her legs," Ty assumed, hitting it right on the money.

Sovanna smirked, and that's all the confirmation they needed.

Although she wanted to leave right away and use the key Zahir had given her, Sovanna kicked it for another thirty minutes before their driver pulled up. She wasn't sure about the classifications of a one-night stand or how it was supposed to go, but entering that man's room without showering first wasn't going to fly. Thankfully, she didn't live too far from the hotel. Once she took a shower, slipped into a comfy two-piece lounge set, and some slides, she was back out the door.

"Did you make it?" Rea asked, yawning into the phone.

"Yes. I'm pulling into valet now."

"Okay, good. Be safe, and don't forget to do what we said."

Climbing out of her Benz, she handed her fob over to the valet assistant and thanked him.

"I won't. I'll text the chat when I leave."

Rea chuckled and yawned again. "If you leave. Love you."

Playfully, Sovanna rolled her eyes. She had every intention of fulfilling her needs and going the hell home. Spending the night was not on the menu. She told Rea she loved her too before sliding her phone into her crossbody purse. Familiar with the hotel's layout, Sovanna located the elevator and climbed on.

Only two locations in the hotel warranted her to use the key in her hand.

A presidential suite.

She was curious to know what he did. The price of the rooms for a night wasn't cheap at all.

Sovanna held the keycard against the electronic reader and pressed P. The ding of the doors closing made her heart lurch. Her nerves heightened as she ascended to the top floor.

"You asked for this. Get it together," she scolded, watching each floor button light up in passing.

When it finally arrived at the penthouse, Sovanna exhaled. A small hallway led her to the door, and she wondered if she should knock. Even though she had a key, she felt like it was still the right thing to do. Just in case Zahir had some other shit going on, she wanted to make her arrival known and not walk in on something that would undoubtedly ruin her night.

Sovanna knocked three times.

Zahir opened the door seven seconds later, greeting her with an appreciative smile. He was grateful for her presence; she didn't have to show up.

"You made it," Zahir acknowledged.

"Barely," Sovanna replied with a chuckle.

Detecting her nervousness, Zahir gave her a reassuring smile. "Come on in."

She walked through the door into a small foyer, which housed a long mirror with two chairs, before entering the main dining area and living room. The open floor plan and panoramic views of the city always took her breath away. While she took in her view, Zahir took in her. Seeing her in those thin lounge clothes made him conclude that Sovanna looked good in anything she wore. He hadn't seen her in much, but that didn't matter.

"Would you like a drink?" He asked.

Sovanna turned to face him and bit into her bottom lip. His shirt was unbuttoned, displaying a white tank covering what she knew was a rock-solid frame. She got a good feel when he pressed up against her in the office.

"No, I'm fine."

"Yes, you are," Zahir complimented, walking over to the bar.

He poured two fingers full of Remy and drank slowly. Sovanna had never wanted to be anything other than a human being until right now with the way his lips graced the glass. When he licked them before sitting his drink down, her pussy thumped with excitement.

"Your fine ass mind telling me how I got so lucky tonight?"

She smiled. "Right place, right time."

"Yet, you're standing over there like you don't know what you came here for."

Sovanna swallowed hard, watching Zahir down the remainder of the brown liquor. His gaze was intense, eyes holding a hint of mischief. He was testing her. She hadn't come this far to not follow through on her dare.

Walking to him, Sovanna smiled as she looked upward. "Better?"

Zahir pulled her against him by the waist. "Much better."

His large hand on the small of her back pebbled her nipples. With no bra on, Zahir felt the second they hardened, awakening his dick. Sovanna's eyes bulged as his member tinted his jeans.

"I heard I was in good hands," she said flirtatiously.

"You heard correctly," he replied, taking in her beauty.

Scattered moles that appeared out of nowhere in her late twenties enhanced her features, and he took a quick count of each one to memory. One on the tip of her left nostril, three on her left cheekbone, two underneath her right eye, and one on her forehead. His eyes then zoned in on her lips. The top one had a natural upward curve that made him want to kiss her, so he did.

The back of his knuckles grazed her cheek before he lightly gripped her jaw. Zahir hesitated for a second, noticing the yearning in her eyes. His eyes asked for permission, and Sovanna silently granted it by pressing herself more into him. He met her lips with a gentle kiss until she moaned. Moving his hand from her jaw to her neck, he fed her his tongue. Sovanna could only taste the liquor he'd drank, but she smelled herself on his beard.

I left my mark. She smirked.

Zahir pulled away, making her eyes peel open. Her chest heaved as his hand lowered from her neck to his belt buckle.

"You told me you were bold; let's see," he reminded her while unbuttoning his jeans.

Zahir lowered his zipper, and Sovanna descended with it. The least she could do was return the favor, and she didn't mind doing so at all. In a squat, Sovanna ran her hands over his toned thighs before he lowered his black briefs.

His dick jutted out with a forceful bounce.

No warning.

No respect.

No timidity.

It didn't care that Sovanna was introducing herself to him for the first time. There was nothing like positive shock value. She felt inclined to show it some love. Her eyes glistened with pure adoration. A man carrying around a dick this long, thick, and gorgeous deserved to be applauded. Sovanna hoped he knew what to do with it.

The carnal yearning to taste him washed over her like no other. With a watery mouth, she let spittle coat the protuberant head before taking him into her mouth. There was no need to use her hands, for now. A rumbled groan echoed above her head as Zahir huffed out a deep breath. Her mouth felt too damn good, and he was trying not to lose control.

His eyes crinkled at the corners as she sucked him with slow, torturous aggression.

Zahir was a grown-ass man with a well-endowed dick that Sovanna was taking down her throat like a pro. He had misjudged her, figuring the stunt she pulled at the club was out of spontaneity and nothing more. She was sucking his dick like she'd been fantasizing about doing so all night. Zahir lightly smacked her cheek when she closed her eyes, relishing in his taste.

"Eyes open and on me. I need you to take this dick down your throat 'til your voice is raspy."

Brown, wet eyes, filled with determination, stared up at him. There wasn't a challenge Sovanna didn't take on. She opened her mouth wider, stretching her throat to accommodate his needs. Manicured nails massaged his balls as he fucked her mouth and voiced his satisfaction.

"Damn," Zahir grumbled. "You sucking this dick like you love me."

What the hell? He scolded just as the words left his brain. The fellatio had him talking recklessly, but Sovanna didn't seem to mind. His compliment aroused her even more. Plus, it didn't matter what either of them said. After tonight, they wouldn't see each other again. She wanted him to talk as crazy as he pleased, within limits.

"Mmm," she hummed, pulling him out of her mouth to say, "I do love *him*."

And that was the truth. His member not only tasted good but felt good as well, gliding hot and heavily in her mouth. Surprisingly, its shade was the same hue as the rest of his body, and Sovanna loved it. Not a blemish in sight, only thick veins that she caressed with her tongue. Finally, she used her hands, rotating them counterclockwise while lapping her tongue around the tip.

His grunts and groans of appreciation fueled the beast in her. Her head bobbed back and forth as the sounds of her gagging filled the suite. The erotic noise made Zahir's sockless toes curl against the tile. Bending his knees some, he stuck both hands inside her tank top, cuffing her breasts. They fit perfectly in the palms of his hands as he freed them to get a better view.

"Pretty ass titties," Zahir complimented, pinching and twirling her nipples just right.

There was an art to it. A skill to bring her plea-sure with just the touch of his fingers. Not every man had been gifted, but Zahir had surely been cast as one of God's favorites in the department of talent.

Before she could drain him of his quickly approaching nut, Zahir pulled himself out of her mouth. Displeasure was written all over her face.

"That bottom lip poking out gon' get you everything you want, gorgeous. Stand up."

Sovanna was pouting but accepted his outstretched hand. Lifting her arms, he pulled the crop top over her head and kissed her lips. His hands roamed her dark, silky skin, and his lips followed. Sovanna moaned softly as he kissed down her neck to her chest, suckling a nipple into his mouth. When she whimpered, Zahir took notice and remained there for a while.

"Oooh," Sovanna cooed as he multitasked.

One hand disappeared inside her shorts as he brought her to the brink of an orgasm with his fingers and lips alone. He was playing a dangerous game. One that Sovanna didn't care to take the score of, because Zahir was winning.

"Take these off," he ordered, already sliding the shorts down.

Sovanna stepped out of them, and next went her panties, which were a damp mess. Zahir stripped from his shirts and kicked his jeans and briefs to the side as well, forcing Sovanna to lick her lips. His body, in all of its naked glory, was downright unfair.

He knew it, too, standing there, letting her drink him in with lust oozing from her pores.

"How much do you weigh?" Sovanna blurted, unable to stop herself.

Zahir chuckled at her inquisitiveness. He found it attractive. She claimed she wasn't always as bold as she was tonight, and he was ready to call her bluff. Though strangers, Sovanna felt comfortable enough in his presence to let her intrusive thoughts take over.

"Two-thirty-four," Zahir answered.

She gulped. "Oh."

"That big enough for you?"

His question was loaded. The man weighed seventy-two pounds more than she did. Of course, that was big enough. Sovanna's eyes traveled from the mural of tattoos covering his chest, starting where the neckline of a shirt would rest, down to his dick. She grinned, making Zahir shake his head with humor.

"Mhm. It is."

"Yeah, I bet," he said before swooping her into his arms.

Zahir's hands cuffed her butt as she wrapped her legs around his waist. Her arms draped his shoulders while her lips kissed his neck. She didn't know where he was taking them, but it didn't matter. He didn't seem to break a sweat as he carried her to the other wing of the suite, into the master bedroom. Sovanna couldn't take it all in, but what she did know was that the bed he placed her on was beyond plush.

Her entire body relaxed as she scooted in the middle, biting her lip. Zahir grabbed a few condoms from his luggage, tossing them on the nightstand.

"You running from me already?" He questioned, placing one knee on the bed.

Sovanna shook her head.

"Good. Running doesn't suit you," he told her, coming between her spread legs.

Her back arched as he kissed down her stomach and sampled her pussy again. Zahir couldn't get enough of her taste. Examining her anatomy, he spread her puffy lips, loving the contrast of her dark skin and gushy pink center. He stuck his tongue inside of her once more and rubbed her clit.

"Zahir, please," Sovanna whined.

His head stayed planted, but his eyes lifted. Silently, he urged her to use more words. A gasp echoed from her mouth as his tongue flickered her sensitivity.

"Oh, sshhiiit," she cried, wrapping her legs around his head.

Her entire body tensed and then trembled as she came. Zahir chuckled at the headlock she had him in.

"Okay...okay. I can't take anymore," Sovanna pleaded, pulling his face up.

Her urgency to feel him was desperate. Zahir hovered over her with a glistening face. Seeing the aftermath of his work and the blissful state she was in made him happy to have been of service.

"You good?" Zahir questioned.

"No. I need you to fuck me."

This was the coherence state he needed her in. He'd worry about logic afterward because right now, as she rotated her hips, gliding wetness against his shaft, it was clear none would be needed tonight. Zahir slid a *SILK* condom on, and Sovanna went to turn over on all fours but was stopped.

"Nah. Stay just how you are, gorgeous. I need to see your face."

Sovanna didn't mind that. They had all night to change positions...so she thought. The second he slid inside of her, she lost her breath. Breathing was a requirement to live, and she'd never felt closer to death than right now. Her hand shot out against his abs, and Zahir leaned forward. He held her at the knees, opening her up more to him.

"Oooh, this dick is *so* fucking big," Sovanna cooed and hissed at once.

Zahir kissed her neck and bit her earlobe. "And you so fucking wet. Tight, too," he groaned in her ear.

His strokes didn't speed up, but he fed her more dick. The more inches he gave her, the wetter she became. Sovanna was dripping. She never heard of dying feeling this damn good. Needing to kiss him, she stuck her tongue in his mouth and scratched at his back. Zahir took it up a notch.

Breaking their lip-lock, he lifted and stared down at her. A grimace was on his handsome face as he pounded into her. Zahir wasn't fond of one-night stands. At least not anymore. He had his fair share of them in his younger days and didn't see the need for them any longer. Tonight, Sovanna wiped that thought clear from his mind the second she approached their section.

"You creaming all over my dick," Zahir announced as if it were breaking news.

Sovanna had no choice but to. Their skin clapped as she met him thrust for thrust. Her movements had Zahir fighting the urge to nut.

Though he was protected, the condom he was wearing made it feel like he had on nothing at all. Feeling her contract around him, Zahir shook his head.

"Un, un. Don't come yet," he commanded.

Sovanna's mouth fell open. *What the hell else does he want me to do?*

She didn't know how she wasn't supposed to when he was sexing her like this. Dick this good should've come with more than one warning sign. She'd even accept a damn handbook manual to study or something. She wanted to throw hands when Zahir slid out of her.

Seeing the disturbed look on her face, he chuckled and said, "Bend your pretty ass over."

Obliging with a smile, Sovanna followed his instructions. On all fours with a sickening arch in her back, ass in the air, and slick pussy for the taking, Zahir slid back inside of her.

"Fuck!" He gritted his teeth and gripped her ass before smacking it. "This pussy so good."

"I know." Sovanna moaned, talking her shit.

She threw it back, not missing a beat, until Zahir gripped the front of her neck. Her grip against the sheets tightened as he held nothing back. Pound for pound, Zahir gave her exactly what she wanted. Her eyes rolled as he went harder and deeper, making her queef.

"Oh, my gosh! Yes! Right there!"

"Right here?" Zahir taunted, poking her g-spot.

He was met with the whites of Sovanna's eyes before she shouted his name. Her muffled screams were even sexy. He let go of her neck and trailed his hands down her slick skin. The view of her plump ass colliding against him had Zahir ready to release. He wanted her to get another one first. Using his thumb, he collected some of her cream and pressed firmly against her anus and rubbed it. The new sensation made her clench harder, another climax searing through her body.

"I'm almost there, baby," Zahir announced. "You gon' catch it?"

Using both hands, Sovanna spread her cheeks open more. At first, Zahir was confused and then, it hit him. His dick got harder, realizing where she wanted him to nut. He pumped inside of her a few more times before pulling out and snatching the condom off. On the brink of oblivion, Zahir stroked his dick while Sovanna talked him through it.

"Mhm. I want you to put all that nut in this tight little ass, Daddy," she moaned.

Zahir's semen shot out of him as soon as the

words left her mouth. His tip was so sensitive at her back entrance that his body trembled as he came.

"Fuuuuck," he groaned lowly, squeezing her ass cheek with his eyes closed.

Sovanna made it jiggle and tightened around his tip until she didn't feel him anymore. Zahir laid out beside her on his back; dick still hard. The only sounds were of them catching their breaths. When he could finally open his eyes and look her way, all he did was shake his head and smirk. He'd been told from an early age not to judge a book by its cover, and the saying still rang true. Sovanna was so pretty to him; he never expected her to do the freaky shit she'd just pulled.

"Mmm. That was real good," Sovanna moaned, licking her lips.

Their secretions dripped from her center as she nastily rubbed her clit. She was still bent over, waiting for Zahir to give his next set of instructions. Clearly, that was his thing. She didn't have to wait long. Seconds later, he pulled her atop him and tongued her down.

"You a freak, baby doll."

The adorable sobriquet he'd given her sounded so good, falling from his lips. Sovanna blushed, tucking her chin. Zahir lifted her head.

"Nothing to be shy about. I love that shit. You good?"

"Yes. Maybe," she chuckled. "I know I won't be able to walk for a few minutes."

Zahir laughed. "That's a'ight. I'm about to carry you into this shower and give you a quick break."

"How quick?"

"Quick enough for you to gain some strength to ride this dick," Zahir said and smacked her ass.

Next, he climbed from the bed and made good on every word he'd just said. By morning, Sovanna didn't have a clue how they'd ended up in the living room on the couch with the sheet draped over them. Zahir's arms were wrapped around her in a warm cocoon of something Sovanna felt was more than what it should've been.

She didn't know this man, but the way Zahir mastered her body was terrifying. He knew when to slow it down so she could ride the waves of pleasure, how to fuck her harder and make her scream, what places to kiss to make her writhe from his touch. It was... gratification at its highest level, and Sovanna hated that it couldn't last beyond this moment.

"Zah—"

When she went to call his name and tell him she was leaving, her hand flew over her mouth. Her voice was gone and unrecognizable, having made good on his earlier requests. Thankfully, Zahir was snoring like he was hibernating, so he wouldn't have heard her anyway. Easing the sheet and his arm from around her, Sovanna inched off the couch and stood on wobbly legs.

Her center ached so terribly good that she had to stand in place for a second and just breathe. After locating her clothes, she slid them on and grabbed her purse. Glancing at Zahir's handsome face and bare chest, Sovanna smiled.

"Best dare ever," she expressed and walked out of the suite.

3

"LET HIM KNOW HE CAN STILL CATCH THESE HANDS."

THREE

"I'm sorry. You said you did what?"

Staring at her best friend, Leerah, on the screen, Sovanna covered her face with her hands. Depending on how you looked at it, it'd only been one day since her nightcap with Zahir. She wasn't ashamed of her behavior, but every time she had a flashback of what went down in that hotel suite, Sovanna shook her head and grinned. She couldn't believe it.

"I had a one-night stand, and I'm sad," Sovanna said, flopping down on the couch.

"You're so dramatic. Why are you sad? It was bad?"

"No, and that's why I'm sad. It was so freaking good. I miss that dick already."

The seriousness in Sovanna's voice made Leerah crack up laughing. She looked as if she'd missed a Glam-Aholic drop instead of missing something she only had once. Leerah stopped laughing long enough to catch her breath.

"First of all," she wheezed, then coughed. "Please tell me when this happened because it's Tuesday. There's no way you're just now confessing the lil' freaky shit you've been into."

Sovanna giggled. "You know the girls took me out Saturday."

"Mhm. You obviously had a good time."

"I did. Our last stop was Club Vice. I had no intention of sleeping with anyone, but Rea dared me," Sovanna divulged.

Leerah lifted her brows. "Some kind of dare."

"Right. I mean, we play truth or dare all the time, so it wasn't anything out of the ordinary."

"So, she dared you to choose a random one and have a nightcap. Hmm. She walks on the wild side like me. I knew I liked her for some reason."

They laughed, and Sovanna shook her head.

"I could've denied doing it and paid up, but I wanted to do it. I've never had one."

"I know you haven't. How was it?"

Sovanna smiled hard, showing nothing but teeth before whispering, "I called this man, Daddy."

Leerah's mouth fell ajar. "Oh, honey. He was putting that dick *down*! I know that's right."

If anyone was going to hype her up, it was going to be her best friend. They were polar opposites, but their friendship was solid. It'd been fifteen years of laughs, love, ups and downs, tears, milestones, accomplishments, and so much more. Sovanna couldn't wait to land and see her face.

"I had every intention to leave as soon as we were done, but that never happened. We went rounds."

Squealing, Leerah kicked her feet. This was so unlike Sovanna, so though she was extremely shocked by her girls' actions, she was happy for her, too. Though she claimed her break up with Josh hadn't really affected her, Leerah could tell it had.

Sovanna wasn't a lover girl. Not in the sense that she didn't believe in love or never wanted to experience it, but more so that she didn't offer it without caution. If she took things to the next level with a man, it was because she'd let her guard down, expecting her heart to be well taken care of. Josh had done that until he hadn't. The way he switched up came out of left field, and it pissed Leerah off to no end how he'd done Sovanna.

"I'm happy for you, Vanna, for real. Would you have done it had it not been for the dare?" Leerah questioned.

Pondering for a few seconds, Sovanna shook her head no. "Probably not. You know me. I only like sharing my body with the man I'm in a relationship with."

"And I love that for you, truly. Not every nigga deserves to sample the pussy, but I love that you got some mystery dick, too." Leerah laughed.

And a mystery it was. All Sovanna knew was his name. She was certain he wasn't going around lying about his name like some women preferred to do. She'd been thinking about him since she exited his suite and couldn't shake him. Zahir was haunting her at every waking moment. Thoughts of their one-night stand flourishing into something much more played on a loop in her mind before Sovanna scolded herself.

Dick got me thinking about the impossible. I'll never see him again. She thought.

"I love it, too. Gotta let it go, though. I'll be home in a few days," Sovanna said.

Leerah smiled widely. "And I cannot wait. Me and Landon miss your face."

"Awww. I miss my baby, too. Where is he?"

"My mama took him to the park so I could clean up around here. It doesn't matter how many toys he has in his room; he brings them out here and plays with them," Leerah said, shaking her head.

Her almost one-year-old son, Landon, meant the world to her. To Sovanna, too. That's why she was the godmother. There was no one else, friend-wise, that Leerah trusted more to raise her son if she no longer could.

"Just wait until after his party. Y'all are going to need an extra room," Sovanna said.

"Speaking of his party... you're still helping, right?"

Sucking her teeth, Sovanna rolled her eyes. "Get off my phone, Leerah."

"What! I'm just asking. I know you'll just be getting in town and stuff. I don't want your time to be all tied up with me."

"You sound ridiculous. We've already discussed the plans and they're still the same unless something has changed," Sovanna hinted.

"No, they haven't. Well, not all of them. I just need to make sure everything on this list gets done. The stuff you ordered for his room came, too."

Sovanna smiled at that. "Good. Those shipping dates had me a little nervous. Share the list of stuff you need to get done with me. It doesn't matter how busy I am. I will always make time for you and my godson."

She teared up and shook her head. Leerah hated crying, but it seemed like all she'd done for the past four months was shed tears. Never in public, only in private where no one could see or hear her. With Sovanna, she didn't mind tearing up. Besides Leerah's mama, Sovanna was the only person she could be vulnerable with.

"Okay," she mumbled, clearing the emotions from her throat. "I'ma share it with you now."

Just as she went to her notes app, boisterous knocks came to Sovanna's door. She flinched while frowning before looking at the time. It was past the time for anyone to be knocking at her door, so she had no clue who it was. An uninvited guest was one that wouldn't be getting let in. People knew popping up on her was a definite way to get ignored.

"You having company?" Leerah asked.

"Girl, no. I don't know who this is."

Another round of knocks came and annoyed Sovanna even more. With no urgency in her steps, she walked out of her bedroom toward the front door.

"Whoever that is must really need to see you," Leerah teased.

Mumbling, "right," Sovanna looked through the peephole, and her annoyance skyrocketed to pure disgust. There was absolutely no reason for her ex to be gracing her doormat with his presence.

"Girl, it's Josh," Sovanna groused.

"Ew. What the fuck does he want? Better yet, why does he think it's okay to show up now? Tell that man to go on about his business."

Sovanna planned to do exactly that. It was no secret that Leerah was team fuck-Josh-and-everything-he-stood-for. As were the rest of her friends. She could continue to ignore him, but she was sure he'd already spotted her car in the parking lot.

"Let me see what he wants, and I'll call you back," Sovanna said.

"He wouldn't want anything if he knew you'd just been riding another man's dick," Leerah teased, making Sovanna chuckle.

"Whatever."

"Mhm. Let him know he can still catch these hands. Bye."

Sovanna hung up. Unlocking the door, she opened it so only a sliver of her frame and face could be seen. Josh had forfeited his right to be graced with her beauty.

"Is there a reason why you're standing in front of my door looking stupid?" Sovanna questioned.

She didn't bother trying to hide her disdain.

"You're serious right now?"

"Very," she replied curtly.

Josh didn't say anything, so she went to close the door. His hand stopped her from doing so.

"Okay, wait. Can we just hash a few things out?"

Sovanna looked him over, urging him to speak.

"Inside," he suggested.

With a huff, Sovanna stepped to the side and let him enter her place. It would no longer be hers in less than forty-eight hours, but it still felt like he was invading her privacy. Josh took a look around the empty two-bedroom he used to spend many days and nights at and shook his head.

"You leave in two days and have nothing to say to me?"

She stared at him with a blank expression on her face. He was handsome in a way that made women and their homegirls say, "Okay. He's nice-looking. I can work with that." Not handsome in the way that made Sovanna want to hump his face. Josh was of average height, about five-foot-ten, rocked a tapered low-curly cut, and had the smoothest caramel complexion.

There were a few things that Sovanna found attractive about him. Mainly how well-dressed he was. No matter the number of designer suits he owned and wore, nothing could hide the façade of who he really was. For a man who seemed to always have his shit together, he looked as if he were losing it right now, and Sovanna couldn't care less.

"I haven't had anything to say for over the last month. What makes you think I would now?"

"I was giving you space to think about us."

She laughed, and Josh's face crumbled.

"There's nothing to think about. Especially between us. Breaking up with me isn't giving me space. It was you letting me know that I made the right choice by moving home."

"You wanted to do the long-distance thing, and I wasn't ready for that," Josh recited, using the same words he'd told her before.

"And, like I said, that's fine. You and I both know why you really ended things. There's no need to plead your case or try to persuade me otherwise," Sovanna said.

Seeing the conversation not going in his favor, Josh paced her wood floor in frustration. He wasn't going to admit aloud what Sovanna felt was a slap in the face, but deep down, he knew the real reason, too. He had all along.

"Look, Vanna," he sighed, walking back over to her. "Maybe I misspoke. Emotions were high that evening, and I regret breaking up with you. I'm willing to try our relationship long distance."

"No."

"No?"

Sovanna shook her head. "No, can do. Do you remember the first thing you said when I told you I got promoted?"

She didn't wait for him to fake amnesia.

"You asked me how I got the promotion and why did they give it to me as if I'm not deserving of it. No, let me finish," she said, cutting him off as he tried speaking. "Then, once I told you it'd be out of state for six months to a year, you said, well, there goes our relationship. You had absolutely no trust in us making it work, and I saw right then that you did not support me."

As badly as Sovanna wanted to ignore the red flags during their conversation that night, she couldn't. Before she could list the pros of her promotion, Josh hit her with every con he could think of, including their relationship. Being with someone who didn't support your dreams, accomplishments, and even your failures was hurtful. The sting of his words hurt Sovanna more than the breakup.

Josh reminded her of her father.

A man who Sovanna went above and beyond to please, and it was never good enough. If she had the strength to establish boundaries with the man who raised her, Josh wasn't exempt from the same treatment. They were necessary, and unfortunately, his would be permanent.

"Are you saying I wasn't happy for you? I never said that." Josh argued.

"You never congratulated me either, so that says enough."

Sighing heavily, Josh knew there was no getting through to her. He'd always called Sovanna stubborn, but this side of her that he was witnessing was beyond that in his eyes. All he wanted her to do was give him another chance.

"Tell me what I need to do so that we can try to make things work," he said in a pleading tone.

"Okay."

He smiled. "Yeah?"

"Mhm. Two things. Walk out of my apartment and never contact me again."

His smile dropped immediately. "Sovanna," he groaned as she pulled the door open.

"Goodbye, Josh."

With a shake of his head, he walked toward the door. He tried giving her one last hug, and Sovanna ducked out of the way. Josh looked at her incredulously and crossed the threshold.

"If you change—"

Sovanna slammed the door in his face and locked it. "I won't."

4

"GETTING TO KNOW YOU IS ON MY
AGENDA."

FOUR

"Where did all these cars come from?"

Sovanna's eyes peered around the community center's parking lot, noticing the new arrivals at Landon's party. The three pans of Rotel, along with chicken wings, were running low, so she ran out to grab a few pizzas down the street. Exiting her car, she reached into the backseat for the pizzas. A deep voice she hadn't heard in so long greeted her when she lifted.

"What's up? Let me grab those for you."

She handed the boxes over without protest and smiled. "Well, look who it is. Mr. Saleem with the big dreams," she teased, pulling an old nickname on him. "How are you?" Sovanna asked, accepting his hug.

"I'm living. Can't complain. You back in town for good?"

She shook her head. "No. Just here for work."

Saleem bobbed his head. "That's what's up. You lookin' good."

His words were far from flirtatious. They never were. Saleem was a good friend of theirs since high school and well into college. Back then, he and a few other men in their circle were the big brothers who took their title seriously in Leerah, Sovanna's, and their other female friends' lives.

They hadn't kept in touch as frequently over the years, but the love was still there.

"Thank you. I see you haven't cut that hair yet," she said, eyeing his two silky braids to the back.

The girls at their high school used to go crazy over his black, curly, thick tresses that draped down his back. "*Ooh. Saleem, when you gon' let me braid your hair?*" "*I bet we'd have some pretty ass kids with good hair.*" Their advances were ignored. He didn't let anyone touch his hair except his mama and then his long-time girlfriend, Amira.

"Nah," he said, giving her a half-smirk. "Probably never will."

"I bet Amira would have a fit," Sovanna chuckled. "She here?"

"Yeah. She pulled up not too long ago," Saleem answered, pulling the door open for her.

"Thank you."

Needing no direction, Saleem located the food table and walked the pizzas over. With extra plates, chips and cups in her hand, Sovanna did the same.

"Girl, where you been at?" One of Leerah's cousins asked.

"Grabbing more food. Look at all these kids," Sovanna said, watching way more kids run around than when she left.

"I know, right? Forget the kids, though. Do you see these niggas? Lil' Landon brought the people out," the cousin laughed. "Better get you one."

Sovanna waved her off. She didn't have time to take in who was present, with kids and adults forming a line at the food table. She'd take it all in once she was settled. On her godmother duties, she went to wash her hands before helping Leerah's mama, Ms. Katrina.

"Hey, ma. What do you need me to do?" Sovanna asked.

Ms. Katrina shook her head, placing a slice of cheese pizza on a plate. "Not a thing. You've done enough. Grab you some food and eat."

They'd been up running around all morning, so

Sovanna did as she was told. After grabbing a slice of pepperoni pizza and two wings, she looked for Leerah. Spotting her coming out of the bounce house with Landon by her side, she grinned and walked toward them.

"Hi, little baby," Sovanna cooed, picking Landon up. "You having fun?"

He nodded his head and smiled so big, melting Sovanna's heart. She kissed his cheek before placing him down to run around. He couldn't go too far without someone stopping to pick him up.

"Girl," Leerah huffed out of breath. "I am out of shape like shit."

Sovanna cackled. "I see. You said not that many people RSVP'd. This looks like a lot of people to me."

She took in the three long rectangular tables that were filled on both sides and the array of people standing up, mingling in different areas of the gymnasium. Underneath and atop the gift table was filled. At a glance, Sovanna knew the candy bags they prepared last night wouldn't be enough for every kid in attendance. Some of the teenagers were going to have to miss out.

"I was not expecting this many people. Most of them are from his daddy's side," Leerah said, waving at one of her baby daddy's aunties. "I can't stand her. You remember she tried to play me when I first found out I was pregnant?"

"Mhm." Sovanna nodded. "Terrance checked her so quick."

"Right. Talking about is he even his. Landon looks just like him."

Hearing the crack in her voice, Sovanna looked her way. She knew today would be tough, and if she had to pull Leerah away from the crowd for a few minutes, she would.

"You okay?"

Leerah cleared her throat. "Yeah. All of his siblings showed up. Well, most of them. A few are missing."

"How many does he have?" Sovanna asked.

"Too damn many," Leerah laughed. "I think seven. Might be eight. Their daddy was out here doing the most."

The friends laughed, and people watched for a few.

"I didn't know you invited Misha," Sovanna said, speaking of Terrance's first baby mama.

"Yeah. She called herself reaching out to me after he passed and wanted to make amends... for the kids. No matter how I felt about Terrance, Landon deserves a relationship with his sister."

Sovanna nodded, agreeing. Losing someone you loved, especially the father of your child, matured some people. Having her son did that for Leerah, and she was willing to put her pettiness aside for his happiness. Had this been back in the day, she wouldn't have thought twice about inviting Misha. Her daughter, Tink, however, had always been welcomed.

"Look at you growing up," Sovanna said, nudging her shoulder. "I'm proud of you."

Leerah smirked. "Thank you, thank you. You know I've been trying to change my crazy ways."

"Keep it up. Awww, look at Landon posing with Cree," Sovanna said.

Leerah's eyes were already on them. Cree, Terrance's godbrother, was crouched down, throwing up the deuces while he and Landon rocked the biggest grins. When Cree dug in his pocket, peeled off a hundred-dollar bill, and handed it to him, Leerah shook her head. Sovanna looked on as Cree pointed to Leerah while telling Landon something. He took off running her way and Cree wasn't far behind.

"Damn," Leerah mumbled, and Sovanna's brows furrowed.

She'd said the word like only a woman could when a fine-ass man was the subject. Sovanna reminded herself to interrogate her later on. She could've sworn she saw a look of something not meant to be displayed in Cree's eyes once he was in front of them. Leerah fidgeting beside her proved her suspicions.

"What up. 'Preciate the invite," Cree said coolly.

He acted as if he wasn't one of the first people on the invitation list. But that's just who he was. How he moved. Like everything in life was a privilege. To him, it was.

"Now, you know you didn't even need one," Leerah replied.

She grabbed the money from Landon, tucking it in her back pocket. He stared at her with the cutest scowl on his face before looking up at Cree.

"Nephew ain't feeling you pocketing his money."

"Yeah, well. That's too bad. He'll lose it if I don't. Go play, baby. Mommy is gonna hold your money."

Right on time, one of his older cousins came to get him. "Come on, Landon! Let's play basketball!"

"Bro would've loved this. You hooked nephew up," Cree acknowledged.

"Yeah...thank you," Leerah said, swallowing the lump in her throat.

Licking his dark lips, Cree glanced toward the food table. "You ate?"

"I will in a little bit."

He nodded. "A'ight. Make sure you do that."

When he walked away, Leerah blew out a dramatic breath that made Sovanna draw her head back.

"Um. Okay. It looks like you have some explaining to do because ma'am... what the hell was that?" Sovanna whispered.

"I honestly do not know," Leerah said, somewhat fibbing.

She knew exactly what type of time Cree was on or thought he was on. Somewhere in the last four months since Terrance passed, the lines had become blurred. Leerah was confused how her grieving had morphed into temptation, perhaps a concoction of them both that was a lethal concoction she needed to stay away from.

"Mhm," Sovanna mumbled. "Girl, it's more people still coming in."

They eyed the door, and Leerah could only shake her head at the abundance of toys the family was bringing in. Whoever had just shown up wanted to make Landon's first birthday more special than it already was. That much was known by the black remote-controlled AMG Benz that rolled through the door next.

"I know this man did not get my baby a Benz truck," Leerah laughed, watching Landon rush towards it.

Sovanna's eyes almost popped out of her head once she saw who was controlling the toy car.

"How does he know y'all?" Sovanna asked, words breathy and almost unheard.

Leerah snaked her neck toward her. "Who?"

"The... the man who's controlling the car."

"Oh. That's one of Terrance's brothers on his daddy's side."

Sovanna swallowed hard just as she continued to stare. "What's his name?" She questioned, already knowing the answer. Somehow, she hoped he'd told her the wrong one.

Leerah frowned. "It's Zahir, why? You know him?"

"Ain't no way I had a one-night stand with my godson's uncle," she divulged in disbelief.

No matter how many times she blinked her eyes, fluttering her lashes, Zahir's presence wasn't a mirage. He commanded every one of Sovanna's senses, rattling her nerves to no end, and he hadn't spoken a word.

"Uh, hello!" Leerah trilled, snapping her fingers.

"Yeah, yeah. What's wrong?"

"You gon' sit here and act like I didn't hear what you just said? *He's* mystery dick?"

Sovanna shushed her. "Quiet down! Yes, that's him. Oh, my gosh. How fucking embarrassing."

Leerah didn't think it was shameful at all. She found it quite hilarious, honestly. Of all the men Sovanna could've chosen to have a one-night stand with, it had to be someone she knew.

"You're only embarrassed because you never thought you'd see him again. Why didn't you tell me it was him?"

"Because I knew who he was," Sovanna replied sarcastically. She asked his name for clarification, not believing she was seeing him again. "I never told you what his name was."

Leerah hummed. "True, and I didn't ask. But whatever. Let's go say hi. If you be nice, maybe he'll let you call him daddy again," Leerah laughed, grabbing her hand.

Sovanna wanted to put up a struggle but didn't. It was pointless. Leerah's offer didn't sound too bad, and the closer they approached, Sovanna wondered how nice of a woman she needed to be. Zahir looked better than she remembered.

Jitters formed in her stomach, causing it to churn once she got a whiff of him. He smelled like money, confidence, and back-to-back orgasms. Something Sovanna knew he was well versed in delivering. Audacious images of him atop her flooded Sovanna's mind, uncaring that she was at a child's party.

And it was clear that Zahir's thoughts had mimicked hers once she was in his line of vision. Their eyes locked, and they became the only individuals in the room. His face didn't give way to her familiarity, but his eyes did. They went from confusion to intrigue, pupils dilating with unadulterated lust. A sure sign that in just seconds, Sovanna had awakened the beast in him.

Her momentary consternation vanished when Zahir smiled, tugging at his chin hairs in contemplation. The way she disappeared that morning without so much as a kiss on the cheek bothered him, and he wasn't one hundred percent sure why but was willing to figure it out. It was maddening how attractive he was and Sovanna just knew every woman in attendance, single or taken, had their eyes on him.

"You came in here trying to steal the shine," Leerah jested, capturing Zahir's attention.

He kept his eyes trained on Sovanna for another few seconds, hating that he now had to focus on anything but her. She was a rare beauty that made Zahir shake his head while thinking, *she's too damn fine.*

"Never that," Zahir said, giving her a hug. "Seems like someone already beat me to it."

That someone was holding her breath, not nearly as bold as she was when they first met.

"How you doing?" Zahir asked smoothly.

"I'm fine," Sovanna answered.

Zahir smirked. "Yes, you are."

Déjà vu washed over her as his compliment from that night in the kitchen of the suite replayed in her mind. Sovanna quietly thanked him.

"Oh. Zahir, this is my best friend and Landon's god mama, Sovanna," Leerah introduced.

Zahir stuck his hand out. "Nice to meet you, gorgeous. I love the name."

She shook his hand and smirked. "They usually do."

His brow lifted, and he chuckled, releasing her hand. "I ain't too late, am I? Got caught up handling some business."

"Nope. You're good. Just in time for us to sing Happy Birthday and cut the cake," Leerah said. "Let me go grab this little boy. Thank you for showing up, Zahir."

He tipped his head forward. "Always. It's nothing but love, sis. Forever."

Leerah swallowed her emotions and scurried off. Terrance was the third oldest, with Zahir being the oldest. Out of all of his dad's children, they'd been the closest, with only two years between them. He couldn't imagine the pain or emotions she was feeling today or any other day, but he hoped she felt Terrence's presence.

Not feeling the need to spark any conversation with him, Sovanna went to walk off, but he grabbed her hand. Sovanna looked down at it, but Zahir didn't release her.

"Loren, is it?" Zahir questioned.

He played along when Leerah introduced them, but now, playtime was over.

"It's Sovanna. But I didn't lie to you," she said quickly, feeling the need to explain for some reason.

"Middle name?" He assumed.

Sovanna nodded.

Seconds penetrated the air until he spoke again.

"What kind of cake is it?" He asked.

Sovanna's eyes swung to the cake table, where everyone began to gather around before landing back on him. His question seemed warranted, but in this moment of all things to ask, that was it? She answered anyway.

"Strawberry and white."

"Damn. That's too bad. I'm more of a chocolate fan. You know, the super moist kind that melts in your mouth."

Sovanna wanted to melt, all right. Right on his fucking tongue.

She cleared her throat, and he smiled. Taking in her appearance, Zahir noticed that her hair was out of the braids she once rocked. It was now in a silk press with soft, flowy layers. Zahir examined her features the same way he did the night they met, and he was convinced that she'd gotten even finer. The images he stored in his brain didn't hold a candle to what stood before him.

"I don't like chocolate cake," Sovanna said.

"More for me. What do you like?"

His question took her by surprise.

"What do you mean?"

"What do you mean?" He said, mocking her. Sovanna tossed a hand over her face, hiding her smile.

Giggling, she said, "I'm for real. Why does what I like matter?"

"Because getting to know you is on my agenda, and I'm a man who believes in handling business in a timely manner."

She didn't want to take his words as him being arrogant. They were spoken so matter of fact and boldly, like they'd been that night. Sovanna chalked up the way he spoke as a man who played no games and knew exactly what he wanted, when he wanted it, how, and where. Zahir wanted Sovanna and he was making that clear. If she needed him to spell it out, he would... right against the lips of her pussy if she let him.

"Getting to know me isn't necessary," Sovanna said, ready to end their conversation.

"I'm sorry you feel that way." Zahir stepped closer, staring her in the eyes.

Her breath hitched when he bent to speak directly in her ear. The measured cadences of his voice were done purposefully, trying to conceal his raw feelings.

Sovanna didn't want to ask him why, but her mouth moved quicker than her brain could stop her. "Why is that?"

"I'd like to think we had a deeper connection than you're ready to admit, and I'd love to take you out."

Zahir saw her body tense at his suggestion. Placing a hand on the small of her back that was on display due to her cropped shirt, he meshed their frames.

"Zahir," Sovanna said softly, praying no eyes were on them.

"And then you go and say my name like that," he chuckled sexily.

She placed a hand on his chest and immediately regretted it. She was trying to put some distance between them and that move only made her want to touch him more. Zahir felt the same way as he clasped his free hand around her wrist, halting her movements. Sovanna couldn't believe they were having this conversation in a room full of people. At a birthday party at that.

"It's coo' baby doll. You don't want me to take you out. I can accept that for now. How about we come to a compromise of sorts? You tell me something you want, and I get to feel you cream all over my dick again. *That* is necessary like a mothafucka," he said with a grit in his tone, gently squeezing her waist.

Backing away from her just enough to see her face, Zahir licked his lips. He hadn't gone one day or night without thinking about Sovanna. He'd had meaningless sex with plenty of women, but that night wasn't just sex. Their conversation flowed with ease while eating meals ordered through room service, and he wanted to experience it again.

Sovanna hadn't shared much about herself except letting him know that she was moving out of state. She rambled a bit about being nervous to start her new job and Zahir reassured her that she was on the journey she needed to be on for a reason. There was minimal talking and maximum fucking in those hours, but enough chemistry had been established for Zahir to want more.

She snuck out without giving him a chance to lay out the change of plans. He knew the moment he slid inside her that one night wouldn't be enough. Now, the stars had aligned, placing them in the right place at the right time again, and Zahir couldn't let her get away. Smiling, trying to keep her composure and not drag him to the nearest room to do exactly what he wanted, Sovanna shook her head.

"As tempting as that sounds, I'm gonna have to decline. We should just let what happened be what it was. A one-time thing," Sovanna said, noticing Leerah waving her over to the table.

Zahir bobbed his head. "I'll respect that. If you change your mind, come find me. The little parting gift you left in my pocket should help you out."

He smirked, and for a second, Sovanna was confused until it hit her. Not the least embarrassed by getting caught for slipping an air tag in his pants pocket when he lowered them to the ground, she grinned. After all, he was a stranger.

"I just might. Now, let's go sing Happy Birthday," she said, walking off.

I need to stay out of this man's face before I sit on it again, she thought. Zahir's eyes fell to her small, round ass, and he shook his head. Sovanna could run from him all she wanted; Zahir just hoped she was up for the chase because that's exactly what he planned to do.

5

"SOMETIMES LIFE REQUIRES US TO DO THE SCARY THINGS."

FIVE

As apprehensive as she had been about moving back home and entering a new position, Sovanna was glad she took a leap of faith. Her first week as the business development manager of Oasis, one of Regal's hotels, an international hotel chain, was over. Her move to Houston had been for a role as a marketing specialist. Over the years, her boss would always tell her he could see more for her.

At the time, Sovanna was still enjoying the work she did and didn't see herself venturing away from her five-year plan. Which she hadn't completely. She'd given herself five years to elevate in the hotel industry, and her promotion came three months shy of the actual date she set. Her granny always said, telling God your plans made Him laugh. Coming back home to Kansas City was her more, even though she couldn't see it yet. With the growing population and status the city has earned over the years, having reputable hotels was a must.

Glancing around the conference table, Sovanna couldn't help but be grateful for her team. They'd shown her nothing but love since being introduced during a video call and had kept the same energy in person. Like her, they were just as determined to ensure Oasis' long-term success and profitability.

"We got a late start today, but we've made great progress this week. Monday morning, I'd like to touch on the idea of partnering with some local businesses around the city. I'm looking to speak with several restaurants and tour operators so our guests can receive exclusive deals," Sovanna said, with all attentively on her.

Nick, the general manager, spoke first. "I like that idea. They'll be able to have a more authentic experience."

"Plus, it'll help us build stronger community ties," Sovanna added.

They nodded, agreeing.

"We can highlight these partnerships in our marketing materials. We all know social media plays a huge role in the growth of businesses. Maybe add in a few testimonials and influencer collaborations," Kamilla, the marketing director, added.

Her mind was moving quicker than her pen could as she jotted down notes. There was nothing like having a team of people who were ready and excited to work. It made Sovanna's job less stressful and gave them an opportunity to actually do the job assigned to them. She'd been in positions where her job description didn't match up with the tasks she was given. She was going to make sure that didn't happen during her time here.

After twenty more minutes of strategizing and a game plan for next week, Sovanna ended the meeting. Heading out of the conference room, she walked back to her office on the main floor. Getting adjusted to her new role only took a few days, but Sovanna knew there was so much more to come. Thankfully, it was Friday, and she didn't have to worry about work until bright and early Monday.

After reading over a few emails, Sovanna grabbed her belongings and headed to her car. It was mid-afternoon, and she hadn't eaten since that morning. Pulling her phone from her purse, she went to search for any new food spots when an incoming call from her mama interrupted her.

"Hey, mama," she answered.

"Well, hello. May I speak with my daughter? Her name is Sovanna Bennett. She's thirty-two years old but not grown enough to not get put over my knee," Alicia said.

Humored, Sovanna giggled. "What did I do now?"

"There is no reason why I have only laid eyes on you twice since you've been home. You really didn't want to come back, huh?"

The sadness in her tone made Sovanna feel bad. Coming back to KC wasn't the issue, it was her father as to why she hadn't been by their home. On both occasions when he wasn't present, which Sovanna found best. She couldn't tell her mama that, even though she was sure she had an inkling as to why her visits had been sparse.

"It's not that. I've just been getting adjusted to the new place and working. How about we have a girl's day soon?"

Alicia smiled on the other end of the phone. "Like we used to. I'd love that. Until then, dinner this Sunday."

Sovanna sighed heavily. "Okay. I can make that work."

"Good. Your brother and sister will be here, as well."

Alicia made the announcement as if it were a special occasion.

"Is there something going on?" She asked, worried.

"Not that I know of. Raevyn is on spring break, and Ray Jr. drops by every week."

Sovanna grunted. *Of course, he does,* she thought to herself.

"Oh. Okay. Well, I'll be there. Need me to bring anything?"

"Just yourself and a good attitude," Alicia warned.

Sovanna laughed. "My attitude is always good, mama. Please. You need to be telling your youngest child that."

"I can't tell her anything these days," Alicia fussed. "Talk some sense into her while she's here for a week."

She'd try her best, but Raevyn had youngest child syndrome. She felt that she could do and say whatever she wanted, and at some point, their parents let her. There was no coming back from that.

"I'll see what I can do," Sovanna promised.

"Thank you and just so you know, if I hadn't told you, I'm so proud of you."

Sovanna's eyes misted. "Thank you, mama."

"You're welcome. I know this journey you're on seems scary, but that's okay. Embrace it. Sometimes life requires us to do the scary things. Otherwise, we won't know what the other side of that looks like."

Alicia didn't realize how much Sovanna needed to hear those words. They came right on time, like always.

"I'll embrace it."

"We shall see," Alicia teased. "I'ma let you go. See you on Sunday. I love you."

"Love you too, mama."

Hanging up, Sovanna rested her head against the seat and exhaled. The last few phone calls with her mama seemed a bit heavy, yet insightful, and she didn't know what that was about. If it was a sign of something for the future, Sovanna needed it to be a bit clearer. When her phone vibrated again, she thought it was her mama calling back, but it wasn't.

"Let me find out you're sneaking on the phone," Sovanna answered jokingly.

Leerah laughed. "Girl. I'm on my lunch break. How was work? You are off, right? I'm just calling like you don't have a serious ass job."

Laughing, Sovanna backed out of her spot. "Yes, I'm off. We get off early on Fridays."

"See. That's the type of job I need. They're having us work mandatory overtime."

"On a Friday?" Sovanna screeched.

She would never and that job should've known better.

"Girl, yes. Like we don't have better things to do. I mean, the money is nice, but y'all couldn't demand this earlier in the week?"

"You and I both know these jobs do not care. You're on their time and dime. Who's going to get Landon?"

Even though he went to one of Terrance's cousins' daycares, Leerah still abided by the rules. Pick-up was before six, and she made sure she was on time every day.

"He's with his uncle. You know, the one you let slut you out. You remember him, right?" Leerah questioned.

They were silent for a beat before cackling loudly.

"Hoe, please!" Sovanna laughed. "Let's not talk about my extracurricular activities when you have some explaining to do, too."

After the party, Sovanna had forgotten all about the way she and Cree had been acting. Well, not him, but Leerah. Cree was always calm and collected and Leerah was moving like he was her first crush instead of her deceased baby daddy's godbrother. Not to mention how he came to comfort her during a mini breakdown she had while cutting the cake. Sovanna needed the tea.

"Well, would you look at the time? I need to clock back in," Leerah laughed.

"Don't play with me! Are y'all messing around?" Sovanna asked in a hushed tone.

Stopping the microwave and grabbing her left-overs, Leerah exhaled. "No. I promise we're not, but he's been extra attentive and checks on me more than my own family. Is that weird to you?"

"No. I don't think it's weird. It's not like you never knew him, and he just entered the picture. Landon is practically his nephew. Has he tried anything?"

Leerah shook her head, though she couldn't see her. "Nothing, but the things he says and does have me... confused. I've never looked at Cree like that. Maybe I'm just tripping because he was the closest to Terrance."

"Yeah, maybe so. Or... you *need* to start looking at Cree like that," Sovanna suggested.

Leerah almost dropped food from her open mouth. "Vanna," she chastised. "No. That's Terrance's brother."

"Godbrother. They do not share the same blood. I'm not saying do anything with him right now, but if he's willingly being there for you, let him. You never know what might happen."

She didn't know where all this advice was coming from, but she was going to blame it on her mama. Seeing her best friend grieve over the loss of her child's father was something she wouldn't wish on her worst enemy. The way he passed was heart-breaking and maddening enough. So, if Cree was stepping up to the plate where no one else was and being a light in Leerah's life, Sovanna was all for it. Leerah, on the other hand, was not.

"Nothing is going to happen. Trust me. Speaking of letting things happen... what's going on with you and Zahir? Are you going to let him take you out?"

"Nope," Sovanna said, merging into traffic. "What for?"

"I can name a lot of reasons, but I'll give you one. So, you can enjoy yourself. What's so wrong with that?"

The thing was, Sovanna knew with a man like Zahir, she'd enjoy herself too much. She already had and could only imagine what more he had in store.

"I didn't come home to get into a situationship,

Leerah. Plus, things just ended with Josh. It's too soon."

"Girl, fuck Josh with his flat head, too-tight suit-wearing ass. And you mean to tell me it's too soon to go on a date, but you let that man nut in your ass?" Leerah questioned, catching a few side eyes from her nosey coworkers. "What y'all in my mouth for?" She sassed, snaking her neck.

Sovanna choked on a laugh. "I'm not telling you anything else. That was a one-time thing, especially with him."

"Boooo," Leerah protested. "Just say you're scared if you're scared. What'd you just tell me?"

"This is different. I would've never seen him again had he not been at the party."

"Yeah, well, he was, and there's nothing you can do about it. Now, he's going to be on your mind forever 'cause you're too chicken to face him like a woman. I'm disappointed in you," Leerah jested.

"I'm not chicken. Give me his number. I'm going to call him," she said bravely.

Sovanna's competitive spirit kicked in, and that's exactly what Leerah wanted her words to do.

"Nope. I'll do you one better. Pick Landon up from him, and you get his number yourself."

Sovanna went to protest but stopped. She

couldn't even front like she didn't want to lay eyes on him and see her godson.

"Fine. Now, how am I supposed to contact him to pick my baby up?"

"They're at Zahir's mama's house. I'll send you the address and let her know you'll be picking him up."

Her heart started beating fast at the thought of pulling up to his mom's place. Things were moving way too fast for her liking, but it was too late now.

"You owe me," Sovanna hissed.

"Mhm. Get a nut off, and we're even," Leerah laughed. "Love you. I'll text you the address and call you when I'm off work."

"Whatever. Love you too."

Glancing at the clock once they hung up, Sovanna figured she could still grab a bite to eat before heading that way. Her phone chimed with a text from Leerah. It was the address and another text that made Sovanna laugh.

> Don't let your competitive spirit fuck that man in his mama's house.

She hurriedly sent her a reply once at a red light.

> I'd have to go in and meet her for that to happen.

> You better act like Mrs. Alicia raised you right.

Sovanna sent the emoji rolling its eyes, and locked her phone. Seeing Zahir was nowhere in her plans today or in the future. It was as if he'd entered her life and wanted to become a resident. All Sovanna needed to do was accept his application. He'd gone about things all backward, having made his deposit two weeks ago inside his suite. His first impression alone should have secured his spot, but since it hadn't, nor had the conversation at the party swayed her in decision-making, Sovanna hoped Zahir didn't give her a hard time today.

Actually, she would. Suddenly, she was looking forward to the chase and the look on his face when she asked for his number.

"I'D LIKE TO REINTRODUCE MYSELF IF
THAT'S FINE WITH YOU."

SIX

Zahir pulled up to his mama's house to a driveway full of cars. The sight was nothing new, and it always put a smile on his face. Family meant everything to him, and he had a big, blended one thanks to his pops, Vince. His reputation as a ladies' man still held true.

Having four baby mamas and eight kids between them didn't stop the siblings from having a close-knit relationship—one that Zahir made sure of even at a young age. He didn't care that his mama didn't get along with Vince's other baby mama's; he wanted to see his brothers and sisters. To this day, wherever he was, they were going to try to be.

Hopping out of his truck, Zahir opened the back passenger door. He grinned at the sight of Landon knocked out. He was out like a light once they left the trampoline park. Unhooking him from his car seat, Zahir hoisted him over his shoulder and grabbed his bag. Walking by one of his younger brother's cars, he shook his head at the scuff of paint on the front.

"And he wonders why I stopped getting it fixed," Zahir grumbled, entering the house. Walking into the living room, he greeted his sister. "What's up, Ny."

Nya, the second oldest, eyes lit up when she saw her nephew. "Hey. Awww, you wore my baby out."

Zahir placed Landon on the couch and gave her a hug and a kiss on the cheek. "Shit, he wore me out. I be forgetting how old I am."

Nya chuckled. "You are getting on up there. You'll be forty in no time."

"Chill. I got four years, sis," Zahir grimaced. "You ain't too far behind."

Laughing, she said, "Far enough."

Tired of working, Nya closed her MacBook and stood from the couch. She was almost as tall as Zahir, standing at five-foot-ten but short enough for him to pull her into a real hug this time. Nya squeezed him and her eyes tightly. She exhaled, feeling much better.

"You good?" Zahir questioned protectively.

She nodded. "Yeah. Just missed you. How long you in town for?"

"I'm chilling for a minute. Got some business out of town next week, but that's it."

"Okay, look at you. How's the agent life treating you? You know Naheim be trying to keep me hip to all these new artists coming out. I be so confused."

Zahir chuckled. "It's keeping me on my toes, that's for sure. Lots of talent out here, but not everybody willing to put the work in."

As a second-generation agent at Maven Talent Agency, Zahir has encountered some of the most gifted individuals. MTA is one of the most established agencies that represents artists and an array of professions throughout the entertainment industry. Zahir's expertise is music, though he has his hand in a few lanes. If the money was right, the business relationship made sense, and the goals aligned, he was on board.

"You sound like daddy," Nya laughed.

They shared the same mama, while Terrance had his own. The fourth and fifth siblings, Victoria and Vince. Jr. had the same mama, while the last three, which included twins, had their own mother.

"Learned from the best. Where everybody at?"

He asked, just as Makai, the oldest twin came through the backdoor. Nya's son Naheim, the sixth oldest sibling King, and the mama of the house, Zola, entered right behind him.

"What up, bro," Makai grinned as they slapped hands, giving a brotherly hug.

"That scuff on your car. When you do that?" Zahir asked.

Makai sucked his teeth. "That's old."

"Get it fixed then. Look at this dude," Zahir cracked, roughing up King. "You ain't getting no women with your hair like that."

King waved him off. "Pull one of yours. On God."

Zahir cracked up. "Never that. Naheim, you got something on your top lip, nephew," he joked as they hugged.

Smirking, Naheim playfully rubbed at his mustache and chin hair that was more than a few specks now. At sixteen, Nya wanted her baby to slow down growing. She couldn't handle it.

"You see me, Unc?"

"What you been doing to get that?" King asked, making Zola shake her head.

Nya sucked her teeth. "Better not have been doing a damn thing."

"What's up, lady? You had them out in the yard

working?" Zahir asked, kissing Zola on her temple, and giving her a hug.

At fifty-four, Zola didn't look a day over forty. Time had been good to her, with smooth brown skin and golden-brown eyes full of wisdom and love. After having two kids, only two years apart, her body was still in tip-top shape. She'd give credit to her bonus kids for keeping her feeling young and active.

"I sure did. They come over thinking all I'ma do is feed them. Better do some work around here," Zola said. "Look at my DonDon," she cooed, rubbing Landon's back.

"Never knew a one-year-old had so much energy," Zahir said.

"Hell yeah, they do," Makai added.

Nya eyed him. "And how would you know? You don't be around no kids."

"My girl got a two-year-old," Makai smiled.

"Let me guess, you playing daddy?" Nya questioned.

"Stepdaddy," King corrected, shaking his head at his brother.

Zahir shook his head, too. "You too young for that shit, Kai. What your grades looking like?"

Knowing he had to show his brother some proof, Makai pulled out his phone. After pulling up his courses and grades for this semester, he smirked once Zahir saw the screen. He had nothing below a B+.

"Yeah, that's what they better be looking like. Worry about that woman and her child another time," Zahir asserted.

Zola swatted his arm. "Don't tell him that. Someone has to give me another grandbaby around here," she said, eyeing them, especially Zahir.

"You better ask Zahir, ma. My shop has been closed," Nya said.

Naheim grimaced. "Good. I'm the only kid you need anyway."

"How are you the oldest and haven't given me a grandchild?"

Zahir scratched his chin, wanting to give her a lewd answer, but kept it respectful.

"My siblings are my kids. Plus, we got Tink, too."

Nya and Zola smiled sadly while the boys uncomfortably cleared their throats. Terrance's name didn't have to be mentioned for the atmosphere to shift. Mentioning his daughter was enough.

"Yeah. I need to call her mama so I can get her," Zola said.

Despite the differences she and Terrance's mama

had back in the day, they had been mature enough to get along for the children. Vince was out here moving wildly, creating families in all parts of the city and out of state, and expected for everything to be kosher. It wasn't for a while, especially when Nya and Terrance were born months apart. His death hurt her the most. The other siblings were grieving too, but Nya felt like she'd lost her twin even though they didn't share the same mother.

As if he knew they were talking about his daddy, Landon's little head popped up. A long yawn escaped him as his dreamy, light brown eyes swept the room. He grinned so big seeing Nya's face, immediately reaching for her.

"Hey, TT's baby," she said, picking him up. She brushed a hand over his soft curls and kissed his cheek. "You're so handsome."

Landon grinned and tugged at her necklace. Wanting to capture the moment, Zola pulled out her phone and snapped a few pictures.

"Y'all stand next to Ny so I can take some pictures," she instructed.

Makai grunted. "You really be showing your age, ma."

"Boy, shut up and take the damn picture before I tell your mama you have a child."

"Nah. Please don't play with that lady like that. She'll throw a fit," Makai pleaded with his hands pressed together.

"Better stop playing then," Zahir warned, tossing an arm over his shoulder.

The men of the family, plus Nya, all inherited their height from Vince, while the two other sisters stood on the shorter side. Smiling, Zola snapped a few pictures, making funny faces at Landon so he could show all his new teeth. Leerah had been nervous about them not growing in, but they popped up out of nowhere days after his birthday.

"Let me send this to his mama. He's just cheesing," Zola said, scrolling to she and Leerah's text messages.

"He feels the love," Nya said, passing him to Naheim.

It was a bummer he had no cousins his age as the oldest grandchild, but he loved his little cousins. His aunts and uncles, including his grandma, spoiled him to no end. If none of them had a baby, Naheim wouldn't be mad about it.

An hour passed while they sat around catching up. Zola whipped up a quick meal of tuna and chicken salad with chips on the side. Only her grandkids could get her to cook on Fridays. Otherwise, her kitchen was closed until Sunday. Her over-grown kids had gotten lucky today.

"Ma, you having company?" Nya yelled as the doorbell rang.

She'd left her phone in the living room and hadn't checked it to see Leerah's text about Sovanna picking Landon up.

"No. See who it is," Zola called out.

Zahir stood to his feet, following behind her. "I got it."

"Boy," she laughed. "You can't turn your bossiness off for two seconds."

"That's not being bossy; it's called being a man."

The way Zahir saw it, why would he let any woman in the house get the door when he and his brothers were there and in range? Nya could call it what she wanted to.

"Who is it?" Nya called out.

On the other side of the door, Sovanna cleared her throat. "It's Sovanna."

Zahir's brows dipped, and he damn near knocked Nya down to pull the door open. Nya shoved him in the back as they came face to face with the woman who'd been invading his mind. Sovanna's breath hitched. She was not expecting Zahir to open the door, but she wasn't complaining.

His warm smile erased all the nervousness she had on the drive and walk up.

"Hi. I'm here to pick up Landon," Sovanna said.

"A'ight. We'll get his stuff together. Come in," Zahir stated.

Smiling, Sovanna stepped over the threshold and inhaled his scent. She was finally given a glimpse of Nya, who, right away, picked up on the attraction between them. Zahir couldn't hide the smile on his face or the pleased look in his eyes if he tried.

"Hey, girl. I'm Nya."

"Hey, nice to meet you. I love your hair," Sovanna complimented, eyeing her curly half-up half-down style.

Nya smiled. "Thank you. We're all in the living room."

"Okay."

Sovanna went to walk behind her but was pulled back. Skeptically, she eyed Zahir and rubbed her glossed lips together. He looked so good in his navy Polo sweatpants and white crewneck tee, his skin all moisturized. He'd left the barbershop that morning, and Sovanna wanted to add to the tip he gave his barber for getting him together.

Some barbers probably had no idea how essential they were in the determining factor of a man receiving some play. Thankfully for Zahir, Sovanna had a few nice words for him and more if he behaved. She was trying to stay on her best behavior around this man, but the way he was staring her down had her ready to act up.

"Can I help you?" She teased.

Zahir smirked. "You could. Walking in my house and not giving me a hug is grounds for you to get put out."

Her eyes widen. "This is your place? Leerah said it was your moms."

"I'm playing with you," he chuckled, pulling her to him. "Damn, baby doll. What's up? You looking and smelling good."

Sovanna fell into his chest with ease, wrapping her arms around his thick waist. Zahir smelled heavenly and felt even better. When he kissed her neck and squeezed her booty in the cream-colored linen pants she changed into, she broke their embrace.

"Don't do that," she whispered, peering up at him. Zahir bit his juicy bottom lip, and Sovanna closed her eyes. "And *please*, don't do that."

"I'd ask why not, but I have an idea. How was your day?"

"Productive. Yours?"

Zahir stared at her, eyes zoning in on her lips. Without thought, he kissed them. "Much better now."

Sovanna licked her lips, wishing he hadn't pulled away so soon. "You can't just kiss me like I belong to you, Zahir."

"I can't, or you don't want me to?"

She rolled her eyes, knowing she wanted him to do much more than kiss her. He smirked at her faux frustration.

"Whatever. What if I have a boyfriend?"

"That's all-hypothetical talk, so it doesn't even matter. If you did have one, the nigga must be a clown."

Sovanna sputtered a laugh. Josh was indeed a clown for breaking up with her.

"I had one, but we're over," she explained.

"Baby doll, y'all were over the second you asked if you could speak to me. Glad I don't have to take you from someone, though."

"You'd do that?" Sovanna asked, finding his jealousy cute.

"In a heartbeat."

Sovanna shook her head and went to comment but jumped at the sound of Zola's voice.

"Zahir!"

"That's your mama?" Sovanna whispered.

He nodded and guided her out of the entryway. "Yeah, come on, so you can meet her."

Meeting his family, especially most of them, wasn't in her plans. She was told their names at the birthday party, but that was it. At this point, she said to hell with whatever plans she thought there were when it came to them. It was clear none of them would be followed.

As soon as Landon saw her walk into the living room, he ran right to her. Swooping him into her arms, Sovanna tickled his belly and hugged him tight.

"Hi, baby. You being good?"

Landon shook his head no with the biggest smile.

"At least he ain't lie." Zola giggled.

Waving, Sovanna greeted everyone. "Hello."

Appreciating her manners, Zola said, "Hey, sweetie. How are you? You were at the party, weren't you?"

"Hi. I'm doing fine, and yes. I'm Leerah's best friend and the god mommy."

"It's nice seeing you again. My son wasn't giving you any trouble, was he?" Zola asked, smirking. She knew her son all too well.

Zahir shook his head while Sovanna glanced his way.

"Not at all," she answered, smiling.

"If he does, let me know," Makai said, sticking his hand out. "I'm Makai. It's *so* nice to meet you."

Nya cracked up while Zahir shoved him out of her face before she could shake his hand. He wasn't about to play with his brother.

"Are you from here?" Nya asked.

Sovanna nodded. "Born and raised. I've been living in Houston for the past five years but recently moved back for a job promotion."

"Congrats. KC is nothing like Houston, huh?" Zola queried.

Laughing, Sovanna shook her head. "Thank you and not at all. We're not really a major city like that, but we have good spots to enjoy and some of the best food."

"We sure do. What line of business do you work in?"

"Hotels. I'm a business development manager," Sovanna answered Zola.

Nya sat up some with excitement. "Really? I own my own travel agency. Maybe we can bounce ideas and resources off one another."

"I'd love that. Let me get you a business card," Sovanna said, reaching inside her purse.

"Oh, girl. I can plug your number in right now. Here you go," she said, handing over her phone with the keypad pulled up.

Zahir stood with his head cocked, taking in their interaction. For someone who was playing hard to get, Sovanna sure was eager to type her digits into his sister's phone, and he found that crazy. He'd never put her on the spot, though, so he let her handle business.

"Aye, bro. You good?" Makai asked, cheesing.

Zahir waved him off. "Watch out."

"I didn't realize Leerah texted me until a few minutes ago. I've told that girl so many times that she can leave him with me if she needs somebody to watch him or needs a break," Zola said.

"If you know Leerah, then you know how she is." That was all Sovanna said.

Her friend never wanted to feel like she was a burden, even though that wasn't the case at all. Her support system was strong on every end of the board, even if they were a little messy on Terrance's mama's side.

"Mhm. I know, child. It's Friday, and I'm not doing anything. He can stay here with me."

"Are you sure?" Sovanna simpered.

"Girl, you better run out of here while you can," Nya jested. "A free babysitter is hard to come by. Tell Leerah he's fine."

Sovanna chuckled. "You aren't lying. Let me text her now."

After sending a quick text letting her know what Zola said, Sovanna locked her phone. She squinted her eyes, wondering if all this had been a setup just for her to run into Zahir again. Whether it was or not, she still had to get his number. That was still in her plans, and she was going to prove Leerah wrong about her being a punk.

"It was nice meeting y'all," Sovanna said, ready to make her departure.

Nya smiled and waved bye. "You too, girl. I saved your number so don't be acting funny when I text you."

Laughing, Sovanna told her she wouldn't and headed for the door. Zahir was right behind her, making Nya speak up.

"Still doing the bossy, man thing, brother?" She teased.

Ignoring her, Zahir opened the door for Sovanna, and they stepped out onto the porch. He'd given her a pass the last time he saw her, opting not to pressure her for any more of her time, but that was all out the window today. They stopped in front of her car, which was parked behind his truck.

"Your mom and sister are so nice," she said, leaning against the driver's door.

"Yeah, nice enough for her to get your number."

Dropping her head, Sovanna laughed. "Jealous?"

"A little bit, I ain't gon' lie," Zahir said, with humor in his tone.

"Well, lucky for you… I had intentions of asking you for your number today."

His brows lifted. "Word? And what did I do to get so lucky again?"

There were a few things he'd done, but Sovanna wasn't in the mood to stroke his ego just yet.

"Nothing much. I'm feeling nice today. Figured I'd do a good deed to end the week."

Zahir's head tilted backward as he laughed from his gut. Sovanna couldn't help but laugh too, as his was contagious. The type she wouldn't mind hearing beyond today.

"A good deed, huh?" Zahir questioned, composing himself.

Sovanna nodded. "Mhm. You don't think so?"

He stepped closer, bracing one hand above her on the car. She sucked in a sharp breath.

"I think it's the perfect act of kindness. How should I return the favor?"

Sovanna swallowed hard, feeling his dick press into her stomach. "Take me out on a date."

"I can do that. What else?" Zahir asked, sliding his hand up her stomach.

Sovanna's belly tightened simultaneously with her walls. Zahir had only been inside of her one night, multiple times, and her pussy was behaving as if it'd lost its best friend.

"What else, baby doll?" Zahir repeated, gaining her focus.

"Prove to me that whatever territory we're about to enter won't be in vain," Sovanna said.

Those weren't the first words she had in mind, but they were honest ones. If she was willing to see what this was between them, Zahir needed to give her some reassurance.

"Only my actions can prove things, so you'll see in due time. Are you free tomorrow?"

Sovanna shook her head. "No. I'm tied up all weekend. Next weekend?"

"Nah. That doesn't work for me. I have to travel for work."

Huffing, she rolled her eyes. "Okay, so tell me how this is going to work. Clearly, our schedules don't align. You should also know that I'm only on this work assignment for six months."

"We're grown and can make it work if that's what we both want. I know that's what I want. It's nothing for me to come and see you or fly you to me. Is that what you're worried about?"

Sovanna nodded. "Yes. You travel a lot for work?"

"Not a lot, but enough to make coming to see me or catching a flight to see you something you don't need to worry about. Just say the word, and I'll make it happen."

Without Sovanna having to tell him anything about why she and Josh were no longer together, him claiming long distance wasn't going to work, Zahir showed her in that moment that it just wasn't supposed to work out with him. If a man wants you, he is going to come get you or send for you. It was that simple, and Zahir needed her to understand that.

Pushing her nerves to the side, Sovanna nodded. "Okay. We can cross that bridge when the time comes. For now, I'll put your number in my phone and we'll go from there."

Zahir shook his head no. "Nah."

"Why? You changed your mind?"

He chuckled. "Not at all, but you have to compromise like I asked. You're stubborn, and as much as I'd love to bend you over and fuck some acquiescence into you, I'm leaving the ball in your court."

Lust filled her eyes. "You'd fuck me in broad daylight in your mom's driveway?"

"Beat that shit down, baby doll. Don't test me. Give me a kiss."

Obliging with pure delight, Sovanna lifted and wrapped her arms around his neck. Zahir was going to keep it as respectful as possible, but he had to leave her with something. Sliding his hand in the band of her pants, he strummed his fingers over her cotton panties, wet with arousal.

Sovanna clung to him as his fingers entered her. The pressure of his palm against her clit, brushing it with intention, had her gasping and biting his lip.

"Zahir," she moaned softly, staring him in the eyes.

He smirked. "I know. Tell me what's going to happen after I make you cum."

Sovanna gasped as his fingers did some sort of trick inside her. Her head fell to his shoulder as breathy gasps fell from her lips. Zahir kissed the top of her head. The act was so damn intimate, Sovanna hugged him tighter.

"Tell me," he urged.

"I'm...I'm going to put your number in my phone," she rushed out, moaning with each word.

Zahir angled his hand to thumb her swollen clit. "What else?"

"Oooh, fuck," Sovanna cried, rolling her hips. Her eyes fluttered as she tried her best to answer him. "And call you whenever I want to see you."

Zahir chuckled, curving his fingers. "That too. You gon' take my number. Use it when you want to, and let me take you out. Is that what you want?"

Her head bobbed. "Yeeees. That's what I want."

Zahir kissed her lips, adding some tongue while she creamed on his fingers. Her body shuddered as he stroked her through her orgasm like the gentleman he was. She hugged him tightly, waiting for the waves of pleasure to slow down. As her chest spasmed, Sovanna smiled and shook her head.

"That's what I want, too," Zahir said, removing his hand from her pants.

Going inside her purse, she handed him a feminine wipe. Zahir opened it while taking a step back, giving her space to get herself together. He watched as she adjusted her panties with a frown and twisted her pants to fit just right.

Zahir's attraction to her wasn't normal, and he was glad it wasn't. He was used to normal. Mundane relationships with women that went nowhere and held no meaning. Women whose actions didn't constrict his heart, make him work for it, or harden his dick the way Sovanna had. Besides the sex, he knew it was more to her, and he wanted to know it all.

Flustered and ready to cancel her other plans, Sovanna cleared her throat.

"So, um. What's your number?"

Zahir grinned and called his number out as she typed it in. "I'd like to reintroduce myself if that's fine with you."

Sovanna grinned. "Sure."

He stuck his hand free of her scent out to shake, and she accepted it. "It's a pleasure to meet you, gorgeous. My name is Zahir Holiday, and I'd love to take you on a date."

Blushing, Sovanna licked her lips. "You're quite handsome yourself, sir. My name—"

"Your real name," Zahir interrupted, making them both laugh.

"My *real* name is Sovanna Bennett, and I'd love to go on a date with you. Does it come with pussy eating at the end of the night?"

Zahir barked out a laugh. "It comes with whatever you want, baby doll. Just say the word."

SEVEN

Rolling over in bed, Sovanna groaned and let out a dry cough. She knew it wasn't night-time, but it sure as hell felt like it. She didn't remember climbing into bed or how she even got there. Squinting, she rubbed her eyes as they adjusted to the sunlight pouring in through her window.

"What the hell," she mumbled, coughing again.

The multiple rounds of mimosas at brunch had her dehydrated and parched as ever. Day drinking put you on your neck, and that's exactly where Sovanna was. Locating her phone, she yawned after face recognition unlocked it. Going straight to her call log, where four missed calls were, she called the one person she knew was responsible for her impromptu nap.

"You're alive," Leerah sang into the phone.

"Barely. How the hell did I get home, and where are you?"

Giggling, Leerah walked down the hall and inside her bedroom. "I was on the phone and didn't want to interrupt your sleep," she said, sitting on the bed.

"I was knocked out." Sovanna stretched, reading her text messages.

"Yeah, for like two hours. That's what happens when you drink two-dollar mimosas and take shots."

Sovanna's head shook as she recalled tossing back a shot of tequila at the bar. They ran into a few friends from school, and of course, catching up included them getting treated to drinks. She wasn't sure what kind of champagne Iron Horse used, but she had no complaints. As of now, they were her favorite.

"I need to get up. I'm supposed to be going over to my parent's house for dinner."

Leerah grunted. "Have fun with that."

That was the only comment Leerah was going to give. As her best friend of many years, she witnessed the lack of support her parents showed her over the years. Mrs. Alicia may not have known it, but always defending her husband's wrongs and trying to get Sovanna to see it his way wasn't what she thought it was all cracked up to be. Leerah didn't understand it, and she stopped trying to years ago.

Sovanna rolled her eyes and climbed from the bed. Her first stop was the bathroom, where she emptied her bladder for what seemed like a minute straight. Afterward, she washed her hands and brushed her teeth. Wanting to change her clothes, she turned on the shower.

"I'm about to hop in the shower right quick," she announced, peeking her head out the door.

Leerah looked up from her phone. "Okay. I'll wait to leave until you get out."

"You gotta pick up Landon?"

"Yeah. He's with Nya," Leerah said.

She smiled, thinking of Nya and her magnetic energy. Not only had she stored Sovanna's number, but she had also followed her on Instagram. When she posted a boomerang of her food earlier, Nya replied to the story, telling her how good it looked. Sovanna didn't want to think too much into it or make a big deal of Zahir's sister following her, but it was hard not to. Josh's sister had done the same thing, calling Sovanna 'sis' and all, yet she was nowhere to be found during their breakup.

"You know, when people say they're a blended family, Terrance's really is," Sovanna said.

Leerah smiled softly. "Yeah. They are. I'm just happy to know my baby was born into a family full of love and mean well. I just hope they never switch up."

Sovanna hoped they didn't either. "I don't think they will."

"We'll see," Leerah said.

Thankfully, Leerah had placed a bonnet on Sovanna's head before she passed out, so her hair was somewhat still intact once she got out of the shower. Oiling her body down, she wrapped a towel around her and walked inside her bedroom. Leerah was curled up in the bed on the phone. Sovanna wasn't trying to ear hustle as she slid her panties on, but the voice sounded much too familiar, and he wasn't on speaker.

"What time y'all gon' be home?" The caller asked.

"I'm not sure. I'll let you know."

Sovanna didn't hear his reply, but seconds later,

Leerah was off the phone and climbing from the bed.

"I know that wasn't who I think it was," Sovanna said, giving her the side eye.

"Whoever you think that was, it was."

Smirking, Sovanna said, "Okay. Call me later on, I guess."

"I will," Leerah said playfully, poking her booty. "Houston got you looking thick. You trying to catch up with me."

"I'ma have a lot of catching up to do," Sovanna laughed.

Standing two inches shorter than her friend, Leerah's body was the total opposite. While Sovanna could get away with not wearing a bra with certain shirts, Leerah's large breasts would never allow her that luxury. They'd been a nice size before having Landon, but she went up two cup sizes during her pregnancy. Breastfeeding helped them go down a size, but not considerably. Her thick thighs and belly, which had a small fupa she adored, and heart-shaped behind were the result of a labor of love and genetics.

"Keep letting that man play in your ass, and you'll be there in no time," Leerah chuckled, walking out of her bedroom.

"That was one time!" Sovanna shouted, snickering. "I didn't even let him go all the way in." She mumbled the last part to herself and trembled at the flashback of her and Zahir's freaky escapade.

Before she could get caught up going down memory lane, she got dressed. Sliding on a loose pair of jeans and a white halter top, Sovanna combed her hair down. Accessorizing with small gold hoop earrings, a gold watch, and a bracelet, she spritzed herself with perfume, swiped some deodorant on, and glossed her lips. After grabbing her phone and purse, she slid a pair of sandals on and walked out of her bedroom.

Leerah pulled the door to the garage open. "I was waiting to leave until you did."

"How nice of you," Sovanna jested, setting the alarm.

They gave each other a hug before Leerah retreated to her car and backed out of the driveway. Sovanna pulled out right after her with a growling stomach in tow. Whatever she'd eaten at brunch was no match for her liquor consumption. The eighteen minutes to her parent's house was made in silence.

Her thoughts were loud, hoping she didn't have to snap on anyone today. Parking behind her sister's car, Sovanna exhaled and cut her engine. The extra few minutes she took for herself were needed because once she entered the home, she wanted to walk right back out.

"We didn't think you were coming." Was how her brother, RJ greeted her.

Sovanna gave him a tight smile. "Well, I'm here. Hello to you, too."

RJ chuckled and pulled her in for a tense hug. "Missed you, sis. Everything been good?"

"Just peachy. Where's mama?" Sovanna asked, breaking their embrace and walking toward the kitchen through the dining room.

She found her mama at the stove, turning the cabbage on low. Alicia turned and smiled with open arms. "Hey. I hope you came prepared to eat. I made your favorite."

Sovanna gave her Mama a hug and eyed the pots on the stove. She missed her sweet potatoes, cabbage, and dressing the most. Houston had some good food spots, but there was nothing like a home-cooked meal prepared by your mother with love.

"I surely did," Sovanna informed.

"Good. Tell everyone they can come eat."

Entering the living room, Sovanna spotted her father, Ray, and sister, Raevyn, sitting on the couch.

A game of softball had his attention on the TV, but he broke it once it went on a commercial.

"Food ready?" He asked.

"Mhm. Mama said come fix you a plate."

Raevyn scooted the table tray out of the way and stood. "Dang. You can't speak?"

"Hello. Don't act like I haven't been calling you," Sovanna said, rolling her eyes.

"I was busy and catching up on sleep. What, you wanted to hang with me?"

Shrugging, Sovanna said, "Nope. Not anymore."

Raevyn shoved her arm. "Don't be an asshole," she whispered.

"Mama, Rae using curse words," Sovanna childishly snitched.

"Raevyn Nicole, don't start your mess. Come in here and fix you a plate and cut it out."

Grumbling something under her breath, Raevyn pinched her sister's arm but did as she was told. Alicia fixed her plate and Ray kissed her cheek as she handed him an empty one to prepare his own. Once everyone had their food, they took seats on the large sectional in the living room.

"RJ, grab your sister a table tray from the back," Ray said.

Shock settled on Sovanna's face at his words. She

was the only one without a table tray. Figuring he was in the mood to play nice, Sovanna kept her comments to herself and thanked RJ when he returned. Casual chatter began as they ate, but Sovanna hadn't said a word. She was too engrossed in her meal.

"Vanna, how's work been?" Alicia asked.

She drank some of her cranberry Ginger Ale before answering. "It's going smoother than I expected. The transition hasn't been rocky at all."

"That's good. Maybe once things are settled, they'll decide to make your stay permanent."

Sovanna chuckled at that. "I hope not."

"Why not?" Raevyn questioned.

"Because I live in Houston. I'm not trying to move back here for good," she said.

RJ finished his bite of cabbage and said, "What's wrong with living here? The city is expanding with more people moving here."

"And I hope they enjoy everything the city has to offer," Sovanna said, not persuaded in the least.

"More people mean a higher chance for you to find a man," Alicia suggested, eyeing her.

Raevyn chuckled. Sovanna wasn't looking for a man, and if she was, she was sure it'd be Zahir. According to her friends at brunch, the dating pool had piss, bleach, and shit in it. All things Sovanna didn't want to submerge in.

"That's not what I'm here for, Mama. These men will be here like they're everywhere else," Sovanna replied.

"I'm glad you're thinking that way. You don't need to be fraternizing when you're here to work. Stay focused."

Ray's words made the conversation cease. It wasn't just what he said that rubbed Sovanna the wrong way, but how he said it. As if she wasn't capable of multi-tasking or deserving of a love life. She was going to hold her tongue, but she'd done that long enough. Wanting to address the elephant in the room, she placed her fork down.

"Why do you always have something negative to say when it comes to anything concerning me?" Sovanna asked as nicely as possible.

Alicia sighed and focused on her food.

"You only find it negative because it's not what you want to hear," Ray countered.

Sovanna sucked her teeth. "No, I find it negative because it's always something with me. Only me. I bet if Rae or RJ moved out of town to pursue their dreams, nothing would be said. They'd be celebrated and encouraged."

Ray grunted but didn't respond.

"Exactly," Sovanna hissed. "What is it, Daddy? You didn't get to live out your dreams, so seeing me live out mine bothers you? Let me know, because this can be the last time you ever see my face again. I promise."

"Come on now, Vanna. All that ain't called for," RJ said.

Sovanna ignored him, waiting for her daddy's answer. She meant what she said and was tired of being treated like a stranger off the streets rather than his daughter. All he had to do was answer her question, and Sovanna's decision would be made. She'd cut people off for less.

Ray cleared his throat. "As a matter of fact, that is why," he stated, making Alicia's eyes shoot up. This was news to her.

"Before Alicia and I had y'all, I had big dreams. I wanted to travel the world, open my own businesses, hell, even thought about writing a book."

"For real, Daddy?" Raevyn queried, intrigued.

He nodded. "Yep. But with having a family comes great responsibility, so everything I wanted to do got put on hold. Years escaped us, our family grew, hardships came, we moved, there were deaths in the family..., and life happened."

"So, because I didn't ask to be here, I get punished with your toxicity?" Sovanna questioned, making Ray chuckle.

"You didn't ask to be here, baby girl, but you know what, I'm damn proud that you are."

An ache appeared in Sovanna's throat, and she tried her best to swallow it. It'd been years since she heard those words.

"Every single thing you've accomplished in your life, I've been proud of. Even your failures, and I guess that's what scared me the most. I didn't want you to go out there and lose your way."

"It's been five years, Daddy. I'm pretty sure I found my way."

Ray nodded. "You have. It's me who is still stuck on the what-ifs."

"And not knowing how to express yourself. Why couldn't you just say this from the beginning?"

"I'm a prideful man. Ask your mother," Ray suggested, and Alicia pursed her lips.

They'd been married long enough for her to know how prideful. It wasn't as bad anymore, but it surfaced full throttle when Sovanna stepped into adulthood.

"Well, as you can see, pride was about to make

you lose out on a relationship with me," Sovanna let him know.

"I see that, and I want to apologize for every time I made you feel unsupported, unloved, and afraid to come to me. You're my daughter, and it should've never been that way."

Sovanna sniffled. She wasn't quite ready to forgive him for the pain he'd caused, but his apology was accepted for now. Only changed behavior from here on out would tell if he stood on his words like a man.

"It shouldn't have, but I accept your apology."

Ray nodded his head. "Thank you."

"You know," Alicia interrupted. "I think his nervousness had a lot to do with losing our first child."

All of her kids' eyes widened. RJ looked back at his daddy with furrowed brows.

"We had another sibling?" Raevyn asked.

"Mhm. She was a stillborn baby that would've been three years older than Sovanna," Alicia explained.

"I never knew that," Sovanna said emotionally.

"None of you did. We were both nervous to try again, but when you entered the world screaming at the top of your lungs and stealing our hearts, we knew it was worth it."

The exact cause of her stillbirth was never identified, and it used to haunt Alicia for a long while. Prayer, therapy, and the love from her husband got her through those dark days. Then, Sovanna was born. She'd never forget the softness of her baby's tiny hand that she only got to hold for less than forty-eight hours.

"What was her name?" Sovanna asked quietly.

"Loren," Alicia smiled. "Your Daddy named her."

Wet eyes swung to Ray, and Sovanna stood from the couch. Falling into his open arms, she hugged him tightly. It didn't matter to her that they just shared this news with them. What mattered was mending their relationship. For her parents to have gone through something so heartbreaking and traumatizing, she could only imagine what else they'd been holding in.

Now, she had somewhat of an understanding of why her daddy acted how he did, but his trauma shouldn't have resorted to abuse. No, it wasn't physical, but the verbal and mental abuse he projected made Sovanna feel unworthy. As if her efforts in wanting to make him proud meant nothing.

She was glad he spoke up today. Men, especially

black men, were good at keeping their emotions tucked until they couldn't. They masked their pain with more pain, projecting their hurt on others who more than likely didn't deserve it. Sovanna hoped her daddy would continue opening up more because healing had no timeframe. Grief isn't a linear emotion. It's a multifaceted, complex response that no one, not even the strongest person, can hide from.

"I love you, Vanna," Ray said, hugging her tight. "Whatever it takes, I'm going to make sure we get back on good terms. Okay?"

Sovanna nodded, too choked up to reply. She couldn't wait until they got back there because she missed her old man. After wiping tears and finishing dinner, the family made promises to see each other soon.

"I'll be by this week to check out your place ," Ray told Sovanna as they walked out the front door.

"You know where I stay?" She asked, surprised.

Ray chuckled. "I'm your daddy. I know everything there is to know about you."

Grinning, Sovanna shook her head. She should've known better. At the end of the day, he was still a protector and a provider. She'd only gone without his support, which meant more than the funds he was sending to her bank account every week. No amount of money could replace a father's presence in their child's life.

"Sure you do," she chuckled. "I'm glad we hashed things out today."

"I am. too. Thank you for hearing me out. And about you finding a man—"

"Daddy," Sovanna stopped him.

Ray lifted his hands. "All right. Not today." He kissed her temple and opened her driver's door. "Get to wherever you're going safely. You should've taken your sister with you."

Sovanna laughed, climbing inside. Raevyn was knocked out on the couch with a full stomach. She wasn't moving anytime soon.

"Next time. Love you."

"Love you too, baby girl."

Sovanna stretched the seatbelt across her chest and fastened it. In a much better mood than she arrived and with no destination in mind, she wondered what Zahir was up to. He called her before she went to brunch, and Sovanna had sent him a few pictures before heading out, but she hadn't heard from him since. Going to her messages, she sent him a text.

`Want some company?`

She stared at the screen until dots appeared, floating with anticipation for his response. When a message of a map of his current location popped up, Sovanna smirked. Zahir didn't hesitate to invite her to his home.

"I know that's right. Drop that mothafuckin' location."

EIGHT

"Your home is really nice," Sovanna complimented.

She stared out of the large windows into his backyard, which had a massive pool, waterfall, and basketball court. When she pulled into the subdivision, driving by all the immaculate homes, she couldn't help but feel inspired. She could most definitely see herself upgrading and living in one.

"Thank you," Zahir said, finishing off his plate of food. "Had I known you were going to bring me a plate, I wouldn't have cooked."

Sovanna licked her lips, watching him eat. Just like the glass he held to his lips that night in his suite, she wanted to be his fork. He could lick her clean, too. Catching her gaze, Zahir held the last bite of his fried cabbage out to her.

"You know it's bad luck to give a woman your last bite of food," she said, walking toward him.

"Is it? I've never heard of that."

"Mhm. They say the woman a man gives his last bite to becomes his wife."

Smirking, Zahir slid the fork into her opened mouth. The visual hardened his dick and caused this weird sensation in his chest. Sharing utensils was a different type of bond, one he didn't take lightly, but it was second nature when it came to Sovanna.

"I guess I need to know your ring size, then."

His words were spoken with full eye contact, almost making Sovanna choke on the spices. Slowly, he pulled the fork back and winked before walking toward the kitchen. Raising the glass of margarita, he made her to her lips, she drank it in dire need of something needing to quench her thirst.

Following behind him and wanting to pick his brain, Sovanna perched on the large sparkling white island in the middle of the kitchen. So far, it was her favorite part of his place, with its overhead vent and stove attached. Zahir's home was everything but modest. Equipped with six bedrooms, four and a half bathrooms, an in-home gym, and a finished basement, the three-level home was beyond stunning.

"You want to get married one day?" she asked as he placed the clean plate in the drying rack.

"It's crossed my mind over the years," Zahir confessed. "You?"

"It used to be on my list of things I wanted by a certain age, but now I'm not so sure."

Drying his hands, Zahir faced her. "Bad relationship?"

"I wouldn't say bad, but it made me look at relationships and myself differently. My ex and I broke up, well, he broke up with me because I accepted the job I'm on."

Zahir's top lip curled as he scowled. "Nigga was insecure like that?"

"I'm guessing so," she shrugged. "He didn't support my move even though it was only going to be for six months and then tried to downplay my career. Like he couldn't believe I'd been given the chance to advance in a field, he worked in."

She downed the rest of her drink, disgusted by the last conversation they shared. Sovanna didn't want to become a woman who self-sabotaged herself based on the idea of someone else's perception of her. There didn't need to be permission granted by anyone to achieve her goals, and that's what she felt like Josh wanted her to do.

To grant her authorization to be great because her success offended him. Sovanna seeking a new level in life didn't serve him, so he found it pointless. It hurt; she couldn't lie, but staying would've hurt and hindered her more. If anything, her progression in life should've inspired him. Zahir shared her sentiments and scoffed.

"He was definitely insecure. A real man with some shit going for himself would've been encouraging you to make that move and would've ensured it was as smooth as possible. Not just because you were his woman, but because he cared about you."

"Exactly what I said, but that's the past," Sovanna said, wanting to take the heat off her. "What about you?"

Zahir poured him a drink and took a generous sip. "Ask me anything you want to know, baby doll. I'm an open book."

She blushed at the nickname like always. "When was your last serious relationship?"

"A few years ago. She wasn't ready to settle down and become a housewife. Her words, not mine."

Sovanna chuckled. "A housewife? She didn't have a job?"

Zahir laughed. "Yeah, but I guess she figured once she moved in with me and took things to the next level, her place in my life would reduce to that. So, she ended things."

He tossed back the rest of his drink, and Sovanna winced as if she'd drank it. She looked in his eyes for a trace of hurt lingering, and her heart simmered when she saw none. A scorned man was worse than a woman. Or a man who was still in love with his ex. That thought made her want to gag.

"You good?" Zahir asked, noticing her scrunch-up face.

She eased a smile onto her face. "Yes. That's too bad. You don't seem like the type of man who'd prefer that."

"It's not about what I prefer. *If* my wife wanted to stay at home and cater to our children, do house-work, and take care of the home, she could," he shrugged nonchalantly. "If not, that's cool, too. Whether she's whipping up a meal with an apron on, waiting on Daddy to get home, or if she's walking through the door from chasing a bag at her nine-to-five, I'ma love her and take care of all her needs. Shit makes no difference to me. Supporting my woman on any level isn't a weakness to me."

Sovanna could literally feel her pussy dripping as he finished his sentence. Clearly, her girl loved the way he was talking, and so did she. Zahir had done and said a lot of things that Sovanna found attractive, specifically cooking, but there was something enchanting about a man who didn't want a woman conforming to societal expectations. Not like she ever had or would, but still.

There was nothing sexier than a man who loved a woman for exactly who she was, not what he wanted her to be. Zahir was talking that shit she liked to hear. Speaking words that slowly erased the thought of her ex completely. What was his name again? It didn't even matter anymore. He was a distant memory.

"You know what... I think you might need my ring size sooner than you think," she said, making him laugh.

"I hear you talkin'. You want that ring but haven't given me a date yet. Coming over to my crib isn't a date."

"Even if it ends with me riding your dick?" She asked so innocently Zahir had to pull her to him.

Sovanna settled between his spread legs, her

chin resting against his chest. She stared up at him with glossy, tipsy eyes, and his hands circled her waist, crossing at the wrists, trapping her in place.

"What you want from me, baby doll?" Zahir asked.

"I'm not sure anymore."

Her answer was honest, and he appreciated that more than she knew.

"It's not gon' be just dick, I'm letting you know that now."

Sovanna's head dropped into his chest as she laughed. "You've made yourself very clear about that, sir."

His eyes tightened, and he spanked her ass. "Calling me that gon' get you whatever you want, even if you don't know what it is."

"I know I want you."

She lifted on her tiptoes and pecked his lips. Zahir gripped her ass and nipped at her ear before trailing wet kisses down her neck. His touch made Sovanna shiver with need. She needed to feel his hands on her. Ever the mind reader, Zahir's hand slid under her halter top and cupped a breast while pinching her nipple. Sovanna gasped against his mouth.

Breaking their embrace, Zahir ran his thumb over her bottom lip. "Strip for me."

She took his hand and smiled mischievously. Leading him into the living room, where slow jams were playing through the surround sound, Sovanna pushed him onto the couch. Zahir smirked, weaving his fingers together and placing his hands behind his head.

"I don't have any ones, baby doll, but you can swipe the Amex in my wallet."

Sovanna pulled the halter over her head and swung it around. "And what color would that card be?"

"Black."

Ooh, he got money, Sovanna said in her head, mimicking the talented actress and comedian Quinta Brunson. She tossed her shirt to the side and unbuckled her jeans.

"Are you a millionaire, Mr. Holiday?"

"Will it get you out of them clothes any faster if I said yes?"

Chuckling, Sovanna slid the jeans over her hips. They pooled at her feet, exposing her arousal in the gray cheeky panties. Doing a seductive wine to the beat of Sabrina Claudio, Sovanna ran her hands down her neck. Her head tilted backward as she palmed her breasts and tweaked her nipples. A soft moan escaped her, and Zahir sat up in his seat.

Elbows on his firm thighs, with his bottom lip tucked between his teeth and eyes blazing with passion, his nostrils flared. Sovanna was teasing him in the best way possible. Her hands trailed down her stomach and caressed her thighs. When she brought them back up, sliding one hand in her panties, Zahir almost stood up.

He watched her eyes roll as she pleasured herself. Fingers sliding against her slick folds, grazing her clit. Her index and middle stayed there, rubbing her nub as her mouth dropped. Zahir scooted further to the edge of the couch. She tweaked one nipple while her fingers almost brought her to a climax. Her movements stopped when he cleared his throat.

"Come give me a taste, baby doll."

Easing her hand out of her panties, she took a few steps toward him. Trailing her fingers down his nose and down his lips, Zahir stuck his tongue out. He licked his tongue in between the V-shape of her fingers before taking both of them into his mouth. Sovanna's chest heaved as he licked them clean, not missing a drop.

When he finished, Zahir's hands gripped the

cuffs of her soft ass. He placed slow, deliberate kisses down her stomach. Continuing his tour, he dragged his nose across the seamless band of her panties before lowering to her crotch. Zahir's juicy lips met hers, and he inhaled deeply, releasing a sound almost like a growl. Sovanna was panting and weak in the knees.

"Zahir," she said breathlessly.

He kissed the inside of her thigh, venturing to her beautifully decorated hips and ass etched with stretch marks. His tongue lapped at those, and lips kissed those, too. Her booty jiggled as he gave it firm smacks.

"Your body is so sexy. Make me wanna lick every inch of you," he confessed with a needy groan.

He lowered her panties, and Sovanna used her foot to scoot them out of the way. Admiring her naked frame, Zahir shook his head in pure satisfaction. Her mound was smooth and free of hair, thanks to her monthly laser treatments. His thumb teased her clit, brushing the hood back so he could suck gingerly. Sovanna sucked in a breath so deep her stomach sank. Gasping, she gripped his shoulder.

Zahir took his mouth off of her to say, "Get up here, then."

Without any discomfort, he lifted her onto his

shoulders. Sovanna's feet barely touched the couch as he covered her with his entire mouth, locking hands at her waist. She rolled her hips as he ate her pussy like a fucking monster. The damn Cookie Monster. Zahir might as well dress up in a furry blue suit from now on.

"Oh, my gosh!" She groaned, leaning over the back of the couch.

Zahir just leaned his head back and kept right on eating. Sovanna's legs trembled, and her hand slapped against the wall. Rapid flicks of his tongue had her screaming his name, until gentle slurps against her clit had her whimpering. With balled fists, her entire body convulsed as she came. Zahir smacked her ass a few times, encouraging her to get it all out.

He trailed hands up her back soothingly. "You always give me the best dessert," he praised, kissing her puffy lips again.

The aftershock of her orgasm made her spasm before Sovanna lowered into his lap. She crashed her lips into his while Zahir tugged his shorts and briefs down. He lifted her some by the waist, tapping his hard dick against her cheeks before sliding the tip against her slit. Thrusting his hips upwards as she lowered onto him, Zahir squeezed her waist.

"Fuck," he hissed through clenched teeth.

She rode him slowly, letting his thickness fill her to the brim. Strangled gasps escaped her with every glide up and down his dick. Zahir licked up her exposed neck as her back arched, sucking her flesh like a blood-seeking vampire. A hand grazed her scalp, gripping her hair as Sabrina poured her heart out on the track about her love being *that* good.

Sovanna's movements picked up speed. She bucked wildly against him, forcing Zahir's hands to fall to his side. He let her take control. She said she wanted him, and he wanted to see just how much. A game of show and tell reversed, with the prize of nothing but straight pipe. Giving him her all, Sovanna climbed to her feet.

"Yeah, ride this dick," Zahir encouraged as she galloped.

She fucked him faster.

Creamed for him.

Screamed for him.

Her voice would be raspy by morning.

Zahir's name bounced off the walls while she bounced on his dick. Precise thrusts underneath her turned into choppy, frenzied ones as she lightly squirted. Zahir turned her into a leaking, creamy mess.

"Oh, fuck! I'm cumming! I'm cumming!" Sovanna cried.

Her body tensed, and her mouth fell ajar, but no words escaped her. Only a gratified, prolonged moan. Zahir pounded into her, watching her make the sexiest fuck faces. He couldn't hold his nut back any longer. His legs stretched out and tightened as he released inside her warmth. Their foreheads pressed together as they struggled to catch their breaths.

Zahir swiped hair from her neck and stared at her pretty face. She looked thoroughly fucked and so sweet but was so nasty, and he loved it. Her nickname came easy to him.

"091287," Zahir called out with labored breaths.

Sovanna's brows dipped.

"That's the passcode to unlock my phone. My jeweler's name is saved under Naaz. Call and let him know your ring size. Ice your ears and wrists out, too."

They'd been joking, but somewhere between her strip tease, screaming his name, and Zahir emptying his seed inside her, the games were over.

NINE

The iced matcha with sweet oat latte creamer wasn't enough to fight off Sovanna's yawns.

It was mid-afternoon, and all she could think about was climbing back into bed. Zahir's king-sized bed specifically. Her impromptu visit wasn't a date, but it did turn into her keeping his sheets warm at night beside him. She smiled at the thought of resting her head against his solid chest while he massaged her scalp. It felt good to just be up under him, asking questions to get to know him better.

After their night of love-making and a much-too-late plate of food, Sovanna thought to finally ask how he'd gained access to the office in the club that night. Outside of being an agent, Zahir had his hands in a bit of everything. From real estate, stocks, bitcoin, and silent partnering in different franchises, Zahir had residual income that would last for generations.

Club Vice was one of them. With Laurent being on tour, and as his agent, Zahir popped up to show his support. Over the years, his roles in the industry have changed. Such as his father's. Vince was a powerhouse of an agent and manager coming up under one of the best talent agencies in the eighties well into the two-thousands.

Zahir took after him. He represented a handful of big-name artists solely focused on his expertise. Sovanna found his lifestyle interesting and exciting simply because Zahir was such a chill individual. She didn't know what to expect from a man in the entertainment world, but she'd heard and read the gossip.

He'd proven her wrong thus far but did live up to one of the stereotypes she and her girls had fallen victim to a time or two. Making good on her promise, Sovanna accepted Zahir's date. It wasn't just a night out on the town for an evening but a trip out of town for four days. He'd been away for work in California all week, missing her something terrible. So, he flew her to him on a first-class flight.

. . .

Last Weekend

Traffic in LA was absolutely sickening, but his presence was enough to dissipate her annoyance. She tongued him down right outside the arrival terminal before climbing into the passenger seat of the Maserati Levante. Zahir was on a business call but was still attentive. A hand caressed her thigh while he pushed through traffic.

"The concert is tomorrow at the Kia Forum. Yeah. Doors open at six, and Kaia goes on at seven. I'll be there right before then," Zahir explained. "No. There wasn't a contract for him, so he's not performing. Tell him I said get his shit together, and maybe we can book him some shows. Yeah, all right. Don't call me unless it's an emergency. Shianne is Kaia's manager."

He listened for another few seconds before disconnecting the call. Placing her hand atop his, Sovanna gave it a soothing rub. Zahir took hold of it and kissed her knuckles, causing her heart to flutter.

"Thank you for flying out to see me. I missed you," he confessed.

"I missed you, too. The thought of sleeping in your bed by myself was torture."

Zahir chuckled. "I see. I didn't get any notifications from my security system."

Along with his passcode to the phone, Zahir gave her a key to the crib. He was prepared to disarm his alarm from his phone before she entered the house, but she never did. Hearing the neediness in her voice, Zahir put an end to the yearning.

"Seeing you in person is better than snuggling against your pillows," she said, smiling.

"I love to hear that, baby doll. You wanna stop at the crib and drop your luggage off or get some food first?"

"It doesn't matter. Whatever works best for you."

Zahir glanced her way, loving her fresh face and hair, which was in a long ponytail. He was happy to have contacts on a few hair stylists because that ponytail wasn't going to make it throughout the weekend.

"You work best for me, and I need to feed you, so that doesn't change," he said.

Blushing, Sovanna said, "Okay. You know... this is considered our first date, right."

"It is, huh? Gotta make it count." He looked down at her wrist. "You like your bracelet?"

Sovanna's fingers brushed over the diamonds, loving how the colors and white light reflected in the sun. The cut and clarity matched the studs in her ear. She put Naaz's number to use Monday morning after Zahir gave her the best morning dick she'd ever had.

"Yes, I love it," she simpered.

Zahir wanted to let her know there was more where that came from, but he'd rather show her. "That's good. You ain't afraid to slide through the hood, are you?"

Laughing, Sovanna focused on him. He wasn't in work mode or attire at the moment. A black KC fitted hat sat on his head while he rocked a white Original Members tee and black sweat shorts. She almost matched his fly, wearing a white tank top, shorts, and a pair of Chanel slides. Her nude pebble mini wallet on a gold chain from Glam-Aholic draped across her body.

"Not at all. You do know I was raised in the city."

"Nah," Zahir chuckled. "I didn't know that. What block?"

"31st and Bales."

Her answer made him nod and chuckle. "Yeah, you were in the trenches. My mama graduated from Central, so I already know you were probably raising hell down there."

Sovanna laughed. "Maybe a little bit."

"I wasn't too far off, though. We stayed all over the city, but mainly with my grandmother in the 40's. As soon as I touched some real money, I paid her house off."

"I know she's so proud of you."

"Yeah," Zahir smiled somberly. "That's my baby

right there."

In that brief conversation, they'd learned a lot about one another. Realizing they had more in common than they thought. They had so much more to learn about one another but weren't rushing it.

Keeping his word, Zahir took her to one of his home-boy's food spots in the hood, and she had some of the best breakfast food. She thought it had something to do with the piece of the edible he slid her on the drive over, but it wasn't. The food was just that damn good.

They spent the rest of the day together while his phone rang periodically with updates about the tour, but Zahir kept them brief. They hit a few stores for her to shop, then headed to his crib for a quick nap. The time difference, full belly, and weed had Sovanna knocked out.

On the day of the concert, she was treated like a special guest and got to meet some of her favorite artists. Zahir scouted out a few artists he was looking to take on and develop while people reached out to network. He gets paid a certain percentage per booking for an artist.

The money was nice and had been lovely for a while now, but that's not why Zahir put the work in. He worked as hard as he did to see the ones who grinded for the fame and had the talent to get what they deserved. It was that simple. If your energy matched his, Zahir was all in.

His newest artist did just that. Kaia put on a hell of a show, making Sovanna a new fan of hers. They spent the rest of the weekend enjoying one another.

If they weren't at his beach house that he rented out to other people when he wasn't in town, Zahir had her in different parts of the city, linking up with a few of his friends, and enjoying her vacation. It was exactly what she needed to scratch the itch of missing him.

Now, she wished she had a few more days to recoup. Her workload for the week was extensive, with back-to-back meetings but she wasn't complaining. This was the life she had prayed for. After a quick video meeting with one of the financial analysts discussing a newly improved loyalty program, Sovanna yawned again and grabbed her phone. A text from her friend Rea perked her mood right up.

> You and Zahir looked so cute over the weekend! Omg. Who knew a silly little dare would turn into this?

Sovanna smiled while her fingers flew across the screen.

I know, right? Thank you! I had such a good time. I miss y'all.

We miss you, too! We'll have to plan a trip to come visit.

Please do. I'd love that.

She missed her girls, and they couldn't believe what had transpired between her and Zahir. Nonetheless, they were beyond happy for her and couldn't wait to catch up in person. A reminder went off on her phone, letting her know that her one o'clock meeting was in ten minutes. After responding to an email, Sovanna grabbed her notebook, iPad, and cell phone and headed out.

Spotting a crew of her coworkers in the lobby, she stopped to speak. "Hey, everyone. Ready for the meeting?"

"Yes. Janiece is running a few minutes late, so I think she pushed it back a few minutes," Kamilla shared.

Sovanna unlocked her phone, wondering how she missed the update. "Oh. She must've just sent an email. I see it now."

"And I see my future husband," Kamilla whispered near her ear. "Damn, he's fine."

Detecting the giddiness in her voice, Sovanna chuckled. Working in a hotel gave them the opportunity to lay eyes on many handsome men and beautiful women. It came with the territory, but not for one second did Sovanna think Kamilla was talking about her man.

When her head lifted, her eyes landed on Zahir and a woman strolling casually down the lobby hall, her chest tightened. Silently, she looked on as they embraced in a hug that was far too intimate for her to be anything less than a woman of his.

But that can't be, Sovanna thought and almost hurled when Zahir kissed the woman on the cheek. Her smile imitated Sovanna's whenever he made her laugh, and she wanted to smack it from her perfectly made-up face. How dare Zahir bring joy to the next woman that wasn't her.

He watched the woman walk away for half a second before he felt eyes searing through him. Zahir felt her penetrating dagger without knowing who it belonged to. When his eyes did land on her, noticing the disturbed look on her face, Zahir frowned. His strides toward her were quick. Sovanna's stomach muscles trembled in sync with each step he made, and he was in her face before she could blink.

"What's the matter? I need to beat somebody's ass in here?" His words were spoken lowly against her ear before he examined her frame like she was an injured child.

Sovanna gritted her teeth. "No, but do I need to beat yours?"

Zahir was noticeably confused by her question. She had no reason to... and then it hit him. A moment of lucidity captured him, making him aware of how what she just saw looked. It wasn't nearly anything she may have been thinking. Before he could explain, Sovanna shook her head.

"It's fine. No need to explain," she said, trying to put on a brave face.

"Let me talk to you in private."

Zahir grabbed her hand, but she snatched it away, stunning him. He cleared his throat, unimpressed by the glares from nosey bystanders.

"I have a meeting and can't be late."

"She's stuck in traffic," Kamilla said, relaying the newest update from Janiece loud enough for Zahir to hear. "Go talk to the man."

Sovanna gave her the meanest glare, hitting Zahir with the same expression before swiveling. She needed to get to her office so she could calm down in private. Zahir walked calmly behind her, the click of her heels antagonizing him along the way, as well as with her body in the form-fitting dress she wore.

He entered her office and closed the door but didn't say anything. The ball was in her court like it'd been. Sovanna's chest heaved as she looked at him. Standing there in a fucking tailored suit looking good enough to rip off his body and purchase another one. The thought of letting him have his way with her while people could possibly hear was ridiculous, but so on brand.

Zahir tilted his head, noticing that look in her eyes. Sovanna snapped out of it. She couldn't believe he had the audacity to come to her job and do this.

"What was that out there?" She asked, getting straight to the point.

"An exchange between a woman I know and you acting as if I committed a crime."

Sovanna's head drew back, offended. "Did you not?"

"Absolutely not."

She scoffed. "So, if you saw me laughing with another man, smiling all in his face, hugging him like I missed him, and then kissing his cheek, you'd be okay with that?"

"His jaw wouldn't be in any shape to place your

lips on." Zahir clenched his jaw.

The thought of her lips touching anyone else other than him had Zahir seeing red and blue lights. He'd be in jail, and he knew it. Sovanna crossed her arms over her chest, drawing his eyes to her perky boobs. She snapped her fingers, reeling him back in.

"My point exactly. So, yes. You did commit a crime, but you know what?" She chuckled. "I'm not even mad."

"People only say that when they're pissed off," Zahir acknowledged. "Maybe I was out of line for showing that much affection with another woman."

"There is no maybe. You were. Who was she?"

Zahir licked his lips and cleared his throat. "My ex."

Sovanna's chest jumped as she laughed. "Ha. Your ex. That's... interesting. Maybe I should call my ex so I can kiss and hug on him, too."

"Don't fucking test me, baby doll."

The grit in his tone had never been used when calling her that, and Sovanna wanted to fall to her knees and pull his dick out. His smoldering gaze almost made her say fuck this argument and his ex, but she stood her ground.

"I'm not you," she said shrugging. "Maybe it was best we kept whatever this was in Houston. I can see now that pursuing something more was a mistake."

"That's bullshit, and you know it," Zahir said, voice even.

He was upset at himself and her for trying to pull this shit, but he'd never raise his voice at her.

"It's not. Fucking you was just a dare, anyway. None of it was real. I was in the moment just having some fun," she said quickly, unbelievingly, avoiding eye contact.

"Do you truly believe that I ate your soul from your body as a game? Taking eight inches of my dick down your throat was a joke to you?"

She knew his words weren't said to disrespect her. Zahir knew her well by now and was positive she was turned on. She was, and it took every fiber of Sovanna not to show him just how much of a joke her head game wasn't. She swallowed down the saliva prepared to help lubricate his dick and shook her head.

"Whatever it was, it wasn't worth it," she said stubbornly.

"So, I'm only worth a one-night stand?"

She pursed her lips and lifted her shoulders. "Pretty much. The longest one of my life," she groaned as if it were a problem.

Chuckling, Zahir nodded. When he stepped her

way, trapping Sovanna against her file cabinet, she sucked in an audible breath.

"You and I both know that's a damn lie. Your feelings are involved, just like mine are. I'm not going to let you reduce what's building between us to a measly quick fuck, because it's not. What I will do is give you some time to get your mind right about me 'cause mine has been made up about you."

Sovanna held her breath as his warm lips met hers.

"Tighten up, baby doll. I'll see you at the crib."

Zahir walked out of her office, confident that he'd be laying eyes on her before the end of the night. Sovanna could front all she wanted, but the truth was the truth.

EVERMORE
SERIES

"Okay, so I overreacted," Sovanna whined into the phone.

Leerah sucked her teeth. "Yes, bitch, you did. Now, he was a little too friendly, but you jumped to conclusions."

Right where she knew she would be, Sovanna

adjusted in Zahir's bed and huffed. She'd gone there right after work to have a conversation that involved hearing him out, but he wasn't home. He hadn't returned home all evening or responded to her texts but disarmed the system so she could get in.

"I did, but you didn't see the way he hugged her, Leerah," she groaned. "It was like he wanted that old thang back or something."

"Girl, shut the hell up! You're just looking for any excuse to end things. Grow up," Leerah fussed.

"Me! You need to grow up and tell Cree that you have feelings for him," Sovanna challenged.

They were quiet for a few seconds before bursting into laughter.

"You almost made me wake this little baby up," Leerah hissed, still snickering while rubbing Landon's back. "I don't have feelings for that man. Please let it go."

"Nope. If I have to acknowledge that this is real between me and Zahir and I was being a brat, you have to take some accountability, too."

"All I'm about to take is my ass to sleep. Call me on your way to work. Matter of fact, just text me because I know your voice is going to be gone.

Sovanna laughed. "Bye girl!"

Hanging up, she sighed and relaxed against the

pillows. She had all day to sit with her actions, and though she was no longer proud of them, she did applaud herself for speaking her mind at that moment. There wasn't a man on God's green earth that could ever play with her heart, no matter how superb the dick was.

She'd been so engrossed in her call, explaining to Leerah what happened, that she hadn't heard Zahir enter the house. Sovanna felt when he stepped into the room, though. His presence tugged at her attention like the night she met him, but it was stronger now. It had something to hold onto and connect to.

Her gaze softened, and her heart melted when she saw the bouquet of roses and a gift bag in his hand. Zahir placed the oval-shaped vase on the nightstand she claimed as hers but held onto the bag. Walking across the room, he leaned against the dresser and loosened his tie as he eyed her thighs. She was wearing one of his T-shirts and nothing else.

"I see you got your mind right," he taunted.

Sovanna's head bobbed. "Mhm."

"Come here and show me."

She quirked her brow, and Zahir chuckled.

"*Please*, come here. If I walk over to you, I'm not

doing any talking."

Sovanna was on her hands and knees, crawling toward the end of the bed. Climbing off it, she huffed with her lip poked out as she stood in front of him. Zahir's arm circled her waist. When she went to speak, he placed a finger against her lips.

"Hush. You did enough talking earlier."

Sovanna blinked slowly, turned the fuck on, but remained quiet. This gentle, bossy ass man knew exactly how to get her going.

"First, I want to apologize for my behavior at your job earlier. There are boundaries that exist when encountering an ex, and none of my actions showed that I knew them. I was there to take you to lunch and ran into her. We didn't end our relationship with static between us, so I didn't think twice to show her the same love I always had. I know better now. It was dead wrong, and it won't happen again."

Sovanna cleared her throat. "Thank you for apologizing."

"Secondly, I know you've had your doubts about us and what we're doing, but don't ever diminish me to just some dick. I told you about that."

He spanked her ass, and Sovanna giggled.

"I was pissed off. You had the nerve to be looking like walking sex and smelling all good, smiling in another woman's face. What did you expect me to do?"

"Take me in your office like you did, and trust that my intentions aren't to hurt you. Not jump the gun, trying to place us back at square one. I'm not feeling that."

Sovanna sighed. "You're right, and I'm sorry. I overreacted out of fear of possibly being hurt in the long run, and that's not fair to you or anything we've built."

"We're good now. But just so we're clear... I *will* break a niggas jaw behind you, so don't ever play them get back games with me." Zahir kissed her lips and handed her the gift bag. "This is for you."

Her cheekbones lifted so high as she smiled that her eyes slit. "A gift for acting up? I'ma have to show out more often."

Zahir shook his head, knowing he had his hands full, and he didn't even care. They were large enough to take on anything she threw his way. Removing the black tissue paper from the bag, her eyes darted to his once she saw what was inside. His head bobbed forward, urging her to take it out. Sovanna held the ring case in her hand.

"Open it."

Her eyes fluttered at the diamonds in the ring

she told his jeweler she loved. They misted with tears as she read the engraved words inside the top.

May I speak with you for a moment?

Those were the first words she said to him, and Zahir loved every word she'd spoken since then. Looking up at him, she didn't have to wonder for long what was on his mind.

"It's a little too soon to make you my wife, but perfect timing for you to be my woman. You mean more to me than some dare and definitely more than a one-night stand," he said, meaning every word.

Sovanna sniffled. "You really got me a ring. This is too much."

"This ring is only the beginning. Will you be my woman, *Loren*," he chuckled.

She swatted his arm. "Hush. What about when I have to move back to Texas?"

If he had his way, she was never moving back. With that thought in his mind, Zahir made a mental reminder to make a few phone calls. Yes, his woman was a boss all on her own, but he could make shit happen without her having to worry. He needed her complete focus on them.

"Let's worry about that when the time comes. I told you it's nothing for me to get to you. I see I'ma still have to make you a believer."

He would, but for right now, Sovanna believed him, and she was happy—happier than she had been before moving back home. The first person she was going to call, or text rather, was Leerah. Had it not been for her popping her pussy and birthing Landon, she and Zahir probably wouldn't have run into one another again.

Grabbing the box out of her hand, Zahir removed the ring from the velvet cushion and slid it onto her right ring finger. It fit perfectly, and he couldn't wait to ice her left one out when the time came. Wiggling it, Sovanna smiled. She wrapped her arms around his neck while he cuffed her booty and massaged it.

"You like it?" He asked, and she nodded.

"Yes, I love it. Thank you so much, baby."

"So, that means you're mine?"

She nodded. "Mhm. I'm your woman. Now, what was the passcode to your phone again? I think I need to make another phone call."

Laughing, Zahir kissed her lips, putting whatever worries she had to rest. Even though it was still early in their relationship, she felt safe with him to know that long-distance, demanding jobs and whatever else came their way wouldn't tarnish what they built. Not even an ex-partner.

For once, the idea didn't scare Sovanna. Zahir made it clear that his actions would always match his words. As he laid her across the bed to consummate their relationship, Sovanna couldn't help but grin. She loved apologies that came with thoughtful gifts, outstanding head, superb dick, and changed behavior. Her one bold move turned spur of the moment, one-night stand, had become a forever thing. She wasn't mad about it, and neither was Zahir as he slid deeply inside of her.

"Gotdamn, baby doll. That's it. Let your man in," he groaned, making her gasp.

If given another chance, Zahir would walk her to his office and take her up on her offer time and time again.

AFTERWORD

Sovanna and Zahir were a time, weren't they? I hope you enjoyed this introduction to the Evermore Series and if so, please leave a review and tell a reader friend. I truly appreciate your support!
Until next month, Love Bri!

ACKNOWLEDGMENTS

All praise to the Man above for blessing me with a gift and allowing me to share it with the world. I'm forever grateful!

Thank you to every reader who supports me!

To my cover reveal and ARC team, you don't know how much I appreciate you! Thank you for going above and beyond for me. Prepare yourselves for the rest of the year!

To my SisterFriend... thank you for coming through in the clutch! I love you!

DISCUSSION QUESTIONS

Would you have gone through with the dare?

Was Sovanna right for putting Josh in his place?

Should Sovanna have folded for Zahir at the birthday party?

Do you think Zahir was too straightforward?

Would you have forgiven your dad?

Was Zahir's apology good enough?

Do you think Cree and Leerah have something going on?